Definitely Earned It

ISBN: 979-8-9954620-0-2

ISBN: 979-8-9954620-1-9

Contents

Definitely Earned It

A Novel

Janelle Lenore

VICTORY SZN

For my mother, Debra.

For my sister, Shavaughn.

For my grandmothers, Mary and Myttie.

For Aunt Jacqui and Aunt Monique.

For Chyane.

For Soror Marja and Soror Jill.

You are the epitome of Black, educated, successful women.

Your strength, brilliance, grace, and resilience inspire me every single day.

Author's Note

This novel contains mature themes, explicit language, and sexual situations intended for adult readers.

Prologue

RONALD REAGAN WASHINGTON NATIONAL AIRPORT – ARLINGTON, VIRGINIA

Puerto Rico doesn't owe me a damn thing.

That trip gave me exactly what I needed, and then some. After years of late nights hitting the books, group projects that felt like unpaid labor, and a thesis that almost took me out mentally, I finally let myself exhale. I drank margaritas for breakfast, lunch, and dinner. I had shots on the beach, and I had shots in my hotel room. I was in my beach chair, laid out under the sun, skin glowing, mind empty, while a fine Puerto Rican Papi fed me grapes. He didn't speak perfect English, and I didn't feel like translating anything. As long as he kept walking past me with his shirt off, we were fluent in the same language as far as I was concerned.

I snorkeled in La Cordillera and watched different fish move in perfect formation. I've never seen so many fish with such vibrant colors. I walked around the town and did some pretty interesting tours.

The trip wasn't an escape. It was a victory lap. Because... I really did that shit.

I earned two degrees, one from an Ivy League, might I add. I didn't take any shortcuts or handouts; it was all discipline, audacity, and a level of cognitive endurance that still surprises me when I think about it. Now that school is officially behind me, my actual life is standing in front of me. It's like the game of life has now said, *Okay, Amina, your move.*

I made the decision to cut off all the men I was entertaining as soon as graduation was over. Not because of heartbreak or bitterness, but because romance is not the assignment right now. Besides, these men are anything but romantic.

I'm not looking for love right now. I've always had my choice of men, but most of them don't keep my interest long enough to matter. Right now, I'm too focused, too clear on what I want, to get distracted by these men. Still, I know myself. If the right man came along, maybe I'd reconsider. I doubt that will happen, though. Right now, the assignment is gaining stability and finding a job.

So, I'm headed back to Amberline Heights to start this next chapter. It's not glamorous, but it's strategic. Amberline Heights is one of those places that quietly produces greatness. It's a Black enclave just outside of Washington D.C. Sure, some parts are a little hood, but there are so many Black people here who have achieved great levels of success.

I did consider starting over somewhere else, like Charlotte or Atlanta, but I don't think now is the time. The D.C. Metro area is primed for opportunities for people who look like me, and I want to take advantage of it. This city rewards preparation, and I've been preparing my entire life. It made more sense to plant myself here than to chase novelty for the sake of reinvention somewhere else.

As I roll my suitcase out of the airport to wait for my ride, I feel that familiar mix of nerves and anticipation tingle through my body. I know this is the feeling that typically comes when one chapter closes, and the next one starts.

I don't know exactly what's waiting for me in this chapter of life. I don't even know if I'm truly ready for it. But it doesn't matter, because I am embarking on this new chapter, whether I'm ready for it or not. Life doesn't wait for anyone.

"Excuse me, miss. Are you, Amina?"

I look up, adjusting the grip on the handle of my suitcase. Looks like this is my ride.

"Yes," I say. "That's me."

And just like that, everything begins.

1

The Wait

Waiting is hard. Especially when I feel like I've been waiting my entire life for this moment. The one where everything clicks, and all the effort and hard work I put in over the years suddenly seems worth it. The one where I can stand on my own two feet, make my own money, and decorate my own little apartment. Once I get my apartment, I'm going to drink hella wine, walk around in my silk pajamas with no bra on, and live my own little peaceful, happy, grown woman life.

Is that too much to expect? It sure as hell seems like it sometimes. Some days, it feels like peace and stability are luxuries instead of basic rights.

Let's be real, I did everything I was supposed to do from the beginning. I followed the blueprint exactly the way *they* said I should. I showed up early, stayed disciplined, and kept my eyes locked in on the long game. I'm practically a professional at doing the right thing. It may be a little arrogant, but... I feel like there is no one more deserving than me. I've been committed to my future since day one, believing that discipline would eventually turn into my salvation.

Honor Roll every quarter in high school.

Check.

Captain of the track team.

Check.

STEM education, stacked with plenty of extracurricular activities, including community service.

Check.

I got A full ride to Brown University, a prominent PWI, because my broke ass needed it, or I wouldn't have been able to afford to go.

Check.

I graduated and came home, then went to a prominent HBCU for grad school.

Check.

I stayed out of jail.

Check.

I didn't become a drug addict.

Check.

I dodged teenage pregnancy.

Check.

I did all that well-rounded scholar bullshit, and stayed the freaking course, despite wanting to quit 1,000 times.

Check.

So yeah, I did that and hit all the benchmarks and targets I promised myself I would. Now, I guess the next step is the one that no one really prepares you for. The one where you get to see if it all was really worth it. Getting your first real adult job and stepping out on your own two feet into this big, ever-changing world. It's really a big deal. I mean, having the education and accolades on paper is one thing, but the idea of putting it all to the test with practical application is another thing.

Every time I turn on the news, all I hear is that the unemployment rate is climbing. College-educated people are struggling, fighting for interviews, and settling for whatever they can get. Some of my friends are working jobs they swore were only temporary, stuck at wages that don't reflect the degrees hanging on their walls.

... I know damn well I didn't put in all this effort, only to make minimum wage.

When I say I need a job, I'm referring to a *good job.* The one that finally lets me get up out of my grandma's house. Don't get me wrong, I love my grandmother deeply. She stepped in when my parents couldn't. She raised me, protected me, and prayed over me my entire life. However, love doesn't cancel out the need for space. She's everything to me, and has been everything for me, but... I need some space. I'm craving peace in a way only independence can give you.

I can't keep explaining social media to her or answering questions about when I'm going to find a good man with good benefits. Not because she's wrong for asking, but because I'm not ready for those conversations to define my life. I'm still trying to find the answers myself.

The truth is, I'm ready for more. I'm ready for growth and exploration. I'm ready to learn, not by enrolling in another course or collecting another degree, but by figuring out who I am as a woman standing on my own. I want growth without distractions, without constant noise, without everyone else's expectations crowding my head. Everyone just sees me as the one who will save the day.

Being the quote-unquote smart one in the family comes with its own kind of pressure and consequences. Somehow, graduating from the *white* school automatically made me the family's financial savior.

Suddenly, I'm expected to have all the answers, all the solutions, and all the stability.

The problem is, I don't have all the answers, and I'm tired of pretending that I do.

I'm supposed to fix my brother's credit. I'm supposed to find the cure for cancer. I'm supposed to travel to the moon, discover a new planet, and somehow still have all my other shit figured out. I'm supposed to be the one to end generational poverty and curses, all while funding my cousin's rap dream, babysitting my sibling's kids, and maintaining my sanity, all at the same damn time.

And it never stops. The reality is, all bets are on me. I feel like it's game six every day. Instead of playing ball, I'm playing the game of life.

See, my mom had me when she was just seventeen. Well, actually, she had my brother Ahmad and me at seventeen. We're twins, but I like to say he's naughty and I'm nice. We're complete opposites, and sometimes I wonder how we spent nine months in the same womb, at the same time, and still came out so different.

Then, there's my little sister, Aaliyah. She's only a year younger than Ahmad and me. Of course, our mom didn't waste any time. Aaliyah started messing with this dude named Braylon, fell in love, and moved to Atlanta three years ago. She isn't doing much with herself down there, but she's always calling my grandmother asking for money because Braylon can't seem to keep a damn job or adequately take care of her as a man.

And then there's the baby, my baby brother Akil. Akil is my pride and joy. He's five years younger than Ahmad and me. Akil, unfortunately, has been in and out of jail since he was fourteen. He just turned nineteen three weeks ago. I haven't seen him much lately, but I hope one day that'll change.

See, when I was twelve, everything changed.

My mom... My mom left home one day and never came back. She died.

One day, she was my sweet, loving, hardworking mom. She was probably overworked and stressed from raising all of us, but she still always found a way to stay positive. She was funny and always smiling. She used to smell so divine, like warm cocoa butter and honey. I can still remember her scent.

And then, she was just gone.

They said she had a bad batch and overdosed. You know how it goes. When I was coming up, people didn't talk much about addiction and mental health, especially where I'm from. Growing up outside of Washington D.C., in Amberline Heights, it was just something you saw, not something you named. I knew she smoked a little weed here and there, but it never occurred to me that she was experimenting with something stronger.

All I know is that whatever she took that day took something from me and my siblings that never came back. Those drugs didn't just take her soul, they took the woman who carried us in her womb for nine months, the woman who loved us, protected us, and believed in us. The woman who was supposed to be our safe place and our guiding light. I know the easy answer is to say it was the drugs, but that explanation has never been enough for me. What I always wonder is what compelled her to do drugs anyway. I've led myself to believe that the world swallowed her whole, and the drugs were the only way she knew how to survive it.

After she died, the state got involved. You already know how that goes. The next thing I knew, all my siblings and I were sitting in the backseat of a social worker's car, with trash bags full of our clothes. Not suitcases, just big ass black trash bags, because that's how quickly everything fell apart.

That's when my grandmother stepped in, or I should say, stepped up. Ms. Jamila Ali, the boldest, most pro-black, and most beautiful woman I know, next to my mom.

My dad, though...

He wasn't around for long. He couldn't be. He was killed when my baby brother Akil was only six months old. One ordinary day, he stepped outside and got pulled into some neighborhood drama that had nothing to do with him and everything to do with where he lived. Six shots ended his life, just like that.

So, with no parents, Grandma Jamila took us in. She didn't have much, but she made sure we ate, and she did the best she could to raise us. My dad was her son. I can't imagine the kind of strength and mental fortitude it takes to bury your child and then turn around and raise his four children. She mourned and mothered at the same time. She never said much about the pain, but I felt it in the way she moved with us, like she was afraid the world might try to take us too.

But Akil... *yeah,* Akil took all of the grief we've been through as a family the hardest.

He was only about seven when everything went down with our mom. At that age, he couldn't really understand that she wasn't coming back. He used to sit on the porch for hours, waiting for her to come home.

He also never got a chance to experience our dad. Six months old is not enough time to form a memory, just pictures.

I think that's what broke Akil the most. He lost both parents before he ever really had them. He's been searching ever since. For something, for someone, maybe even for himself.

So, when it comes to me, being the only one who has positive traction in life, the expectations of me are high.

Every minute, all I hear is, "Amina, can you help me?"

"Amina, can you testify for me?"

"Amina, can you take me here?"

Amina this, and Amina that.

It starts to sound like, *Cinderella, can you do this and Cinderella, can you do that,* like my name has been replaced with a list of errands. I'm not sure if all this pressure is healthy for me. I wonder if this was the same pressure my mother felt.

But I don't complain. I just smile, nod, and do what I can, because complaining doesn't change the circumstances. Complaining doesn't bring my mom back. Complaining doesn't bring my dad back. Complaining doesn't make anything better.

I really want to be successful, and I want to get out of here. That's why waiting feels unbearable. I need something to come through, not as a miracle, but as proof that all this effort wasn't misplaced. I just want things to finally work in my favor for once.

It's been four months since graduating from grad school. Four long, humbling months that stretched me thin in ways no syllabus ever could. And still, nothing.

No interviews. No callbacks. No polite, "We can't wait to meet you," emails to break the silence. Today, I submitted my hundredth application. *One. Hundred.*

I don't truly know if that's normal at this point. Especially when every time I click submit, it feels like my application disappears into some sort of corporate black hole where hope goes to wait quietly. I swear this entire process is a test of patience. Patience has never been my greatest virtue.

First, they want you to fill out an application that takes roughly forty-five minutes. Name, address, references, social security number, favorite color, blood type, blah, blah, blah. Then, after all that, they have the audacity to ask you to attach your résumé.

Like... *excuse me.*

Didn't I just type out my entire resume word for word into your little boxes? What's the point of making someone break their life down line by line, only to ask them for the same story again as an attachment? *It's giving... redundant.*

But I still do it. Every single time. What if this one's different? What if this one is the one? These are the questions I ask myself each time I fill out an application.

So, I submit, sit back, and try not to spiral. It's draining, but I remind myself to stay the course. I didn't come this far or survive everything I've been through to give up now. Somewhere out there, somebody is going to read Amina Ali's résumé and realize they didn't just find a candidate. They struck gold.

I am gold.

Black gold, of course.

Deep down, I know I'm qualified. I am capable. I've worked for this. I've earned this. And even if no one sees it yet, they will.

Until then, I wait.

2

The Offer

Another Morning.

"Amina!" Grandma Jamila yells.

I hear her before I see her.

"Amina!"

Here we go again. This shit is practically every day.

"You ain't gon' sleep all day! It's ten o'clock! Get up, Amina! Ahmad's kids are coming over, and I need you to help watch them," she yells up the narrow steps.

I roll over, burying my face in my flat pillows. I swear Grandma Jamila's voice could cut through steel. It's like God gave her lungs made of bullhorns. *Damn.*

"Grandma, it's ten o'clock, jeez," I slightly yell back, trying not to give her the inclination that I have an attitude.

No response, just heavy footsteps on the creaky old floors in this row house. That's her signature move.

I can't believe this is my life right now. Twenty-four, two degrees, unemployed, and still living at my grandma's house, in the hood, might I add. And as if that were not enough, I'm also the built-in babysitter for my brother's kids.

I love my nieces and nephews, I really do, but they're also annoying. I didn't dodge teen pregnancy just to still be locked down with kids. I shouldn't be held responsible for him not being able to keep it in his pants.

This is exactly why I need a job that will get me out of here. I am the default adult. I am always the designated responsible party. I am... tired.

As soon as I get a job, I will be getting me an apartment. My future apartment is going to be a child-free zone. In fact, I am going to get a sign made that says, *please leave your kids and your problems at home*, and hang it on the door. I don't even care if it's petty.

In my chateau, there will be no toys, no sticky fingers, no nursery rhymes. All those things will be banned in the confines of my home. When I say no children, I mean it.

Ughhh.

I guess I should get up before Grandma comes in here herself. I grab my phone, open my email app, and start scrolling through my inbox.

Inbox: 12 New Messages

> **From: Kiss At Night Radio**
>
> **To: Amina Ali**
>
> Your free trial has ended. Would you like to subscribe?

No. I would not like to subscribe.

***Delete.* Next email.**

From: Amberline Credit Union

To: Amina Ali

Dear Amina, congratulations. Based on your recent activity, you are now eligible for a $100 increase to your credit limit.

Wow, my big break. A hundred more dollars I can't afford to spend.

Next email.

From: FindYourLoveConnection

To: Amina Ali

Are you looking for love? Join FindYourLoveConnection.c om today and meet your perfect match.

Hell No! Delete.

This is exactly why I hate checking my email. It's always a bunch of random shit. Promotions, spam, and a whole lot of bullshit pretending to be important.

I continue reading my emails, then something catches my eye. An email from a Ben Kowalski saying something about an interview opportunity. My heart skips, hard enough that I feel it in my throat.

"Please don't be a scam," I whisper, already holding my breath as I click it open.

From: Ben Kowalski

Subject: Interview Opportunity

Hello, Ms. Ali, I've received your application and would like to schedule an interview to further discuss the role you applied for. Please let me know if tomorrow at 9:00 a.m. works for you for a video interview. Have a great day, Ben.

An interview... An actual interview. Not a rejection, and not silence.

"Oh, my goodness... finally!" I say out loud, unable to keep it in.

I fumble with my phone, trying to type my response to Ben's email. I want every word to be right. I can't afford to fumble this opportunity.

Yes, tomorrow at 9 a.m. works perfectly. Thank you so much for the opportunity, Mr. Kowalski, and I look forward to speaking with you. Thanks, Amina.

I hit send, then just sit there for a second, staring at my phone. My heart is pounding, like I just finished running at a track meet.

Could this really be it?

Oh boy. I can already hear my grandma hooting and hollering again.

"Amina, you hear me? You need to get up," Grandma Jamila yells.

See, this is that shit.

"Yes, ma'am, I'm up, Grandma," I holler back. This time, there's a little joy in my voice, because for the first time in months, something is finally moving.

***

The next day.

It's barely 6 a.m., and I'm already awake. Not just awake, but wide awake. I barely slept last night. My nerves are shadow boxing in my stomach, and every breath feels like it's trying to outrun my anxiety. I've only been out of bed for ten minutes, and I already feel like I could throw up.

Today is the day. The interview.

The one I've been praying for, refreshing my emails for, and begging God to finally deliver. They say, prayer without works is dead, and I've definitely put in the work.

And now that it's here, I'm pacing back and forth in my room like a crackhead, rummaging through my closet with a kind of frantic energy I would usually reserve for my wild bullshit.

It's a video interview, so technically they'll only see my upper half. But knowing my luck, this would be the day they ask me to stand up and grab something, and I'm standing there looking stupid in pajama bottoms.

Nope. I need to look put together head to toe, just in case. Stay ready, so I don't have to get ready. That motto has never steered me wrong before.

My mirror catches me spiraling. So many thoughts are rolling around my mind all at once, bumping into each other like they're trying to escape.

What if they don't like me?

What if I stutter?

What if they ask me something I don't know?

Do they even know that I'm Black?

I stop myself, and a small, slightly unhinged laugh slips out that is half humor and half fear. With a name like Amina Ali, they've got to know that I'm not *Becky from Branding.* Maybe they don't know that I'm Black, per se, but they've got to at least know that I'm cultured.

My hands are shaking now, so I do the only thing I know that calms me. I pray to the good man above. I close my eyes and let the words settle into the quiet space inside me. The one that's always been there when I needed it most.

"Dear God, please give me poise today. Calm my spirit. Let my answers sound confident, even though I'm nervous. And God, please do not let these questions be too hard. Amen."

When I open my eyes, I feel a little more at ease. Not calm, but steadier and more focused. Like God grabbed me by the shoulders and said, "Get it together, girl. You've got this."

I check my phone again. 8:40 a.m.

Damn, it's go time.

I set up my half-broken laptop, the same one that dragged its tired hinges with me through four years of undergrad and two years of grad school. The same one that overheated so badly during finals week that I had to put ice packs under it like it was my sick nephew.

I touch the keyboard and whisper to myself, "God, empower this laptop. Please. If it dies on me today, I truly don't know what I'll do."

I log on early, of course, and sit there waiting, heart pounding and hands sweating, pretending to look casual even though I'm dying inside.

Then the screen flickers, and a box pops up.

Ben Kowalski is joining the meeting.

Here we go.

The camera settles on a middle-aged white man with kind green eyes and a perfectly trimmed mustache.

"Hello, Amina," he says. "I'm Ben Kowalski, Director here at OHE & Associates. It's a pleasure to meet you today."

I swallow hard. "Hello, Ben. So nice to meet you as well."

He nods, smiling. "Let's start simple. Tell me a little more about yourself."

Of course, he wants to start here. The one question that always feels like it should be easy but, somehow feels like being asked to describe the entire universe in under a minute. I have never been the best at reciting my elevator pitch.

The pro-boxers in my stomach start punching me again.

"Well," I begin, "I graduated this year with a graduate degree in Marketing. I also have an undergraduate degree in Economics from Brown. I love cooking... and puppy yoga is fun too." I laugh nervously. "And I'm a twin. Is... um... is that what you're looking for?"

Ben chuckles, warm and unbothered. "Yes, that's perfect."

Relief washes through me so strongly, I almost melt in my chair.

The interview keeps going, with about thirty full minutes of questions, explanations, and details about the role. Then, he says the words that freeze time.

"Well, Amina... I think I've heard everything I needed to hear." He smiles. "I'd like to offer you the role of Junior Program Manager on our Corporate Events Team. The starting salary is $75,000 with a $1,500 sign-on bonus. Would you like to make a decision now, or do you need some time to think it over?"

My mouth acts before my brain catches up.

"YES!" It bursts out of me so fast I damn near startled myself.

I immediately slap my hand over my mouth.

"I mean... yes," I repeat, softer this time, a little more professional. "I'd love to accept the offer."

"Wonderful," Ben says. We're excited to have you. HR will send over the paperwork by close of business. Welcome to OHE & Associates, Amina."

And just like that, the meeting ends. No countdown or drumroll, just a quiet click and a new future.

Just like that, my life changes. This is my big break. This is the moment I've been praying for.

I sit there for a moment, staring at the black screen where Ben's face used to be. My heartbeat sounds like a drumline, loud and triumphant.

I got the offer...

I got the opportunity.

I got my chance.

And for the first time, it feels like the waiting meant something.

3

Day One

It's day one.

In approximately ten minutes, I'll be walking into my first real job. I still can't believe this is the job that might actually turn into a career. Junior Program Manager. Damn, that sounds good. I already know people are going to be sick of me slipping my title into random conversations, but I don't even care. The title alone makes me stand up a little straighter. It makes me feel like a dignified woman.

God really did his big one with this opportunity, because I finally get to put into practice all the things I've poured into myself. The degrees, the discipline, the emotional stamina, and the tenacity I had to pull from places I didn't even know existed.

This morning, Grandma Jamila woke up before the sun just to watch me get dressed. I remember she used to do this with my brothers, sister, and me when we would get ready for our first day of school. She stood in the doorway with her arms crossed, eyes softening the way they do when she's proud but trying not to cry.

"You look like a woman with purpose, Mina," she said.

And I'm not going to lie, it felt good. Like I was finally stepping into the version of myself she prayed for. Which also means, in the most respectful way possible, I cannot fuck this up.

I promised myself I'd walk in poised and observant, absorbing everything like an intellectual sponge. First impressions matter, and today I want to exude competence, eloquence, and maybe the faintest suggestion of, *you're going to wish you hired me sooner.*

Except, I'm currently stuck on this nasty-ass train. Again.

It never fails. It always smells like a special blend of stale air, exhaust fumes, and urine. Every commute feels like I'm sacrificing my respiratory health in exchange for a ride. One thing I know for certain, after I save enough for an apartment, I'm saving for a car. I don't need anything fancy, just something to get around in.

"L'Enfant Plaza. Door opening on the left," the conductor announces.

I step off the train and make the short walk to OHE & Associates, trying not to sweat through my silk blouse. The moment I step inside the lobby, it feels like I've entered another world. The ambience is immaculate. It's modern, sleek, and looks hella expensive. I look around and see curated art pieces all over. Even the eucalyptus scent floating in the air feels intentional, like the building itself is practicing aromatherapy.

No one seems to really notice me, which is... weirdly comforting. Better invisible than scrutinized.

I walk up to the receptionist's desk, and there's this young woman with perfectly curled blonde hair and a smile so tight it looks like it's on probation.

"Hi, excuse me," I say. "My name is Amina Ali, and I'm looking for Ben Kowalski."

She blinks at me as if I've just interrupted a deep spiritual reflection.

"Ben? Ben doesn't really take guests. What do you need him for? Is this a delivery?"

Delivery.

Delivery?

Ma'am.

These heels, these slacks, this silk button-up? Not a single fiber on my body is giving *FedEx.* Silly lady.

"No," I say calmly, though my eyebrow tries to rise on its own. "I'll be working here. Today is actually my first day."

She freezes. I can tell she's no longer sure of herself, like she's actively revising whatever stereotype she had just assigned me.

"Oh. Okay, let me call him. You can have a seat."

I thank her and walk to the waiting area. It's stunning. The furniture is gorgeous, aesthetically pleasing... and hard as hell. I think it's Scandinavian. I swear I've sat on bricks more comfortably than this. Even Grandma Jamila's old ass couch is more forgiving than this.

"Amina. Ms. Ali."

I look up, and there's Ben, wearing the same warm smile from the video call. Seeing him in person, it's immediately evident that the man is tall. Like he used to hoop in his past life tall. I'm five foot five, and I'm craning my whole neck just to greet him.

"Pleasure to finally meet you," he says as we shake hands. He gives golden retriever energy. He's friendly, kind, and he probably packs organic snacks and granola. I think he likes dogs. He looks like he likes dogs. Which means if he likes dogs, he's probably a nice person.

We walk and talk until he stops at a cubicle.

"Here you go. This will be your cubicle in our lovely cube farm. Feel free to decorate it however you'd like. Staff meeting is in about thirty minutes. I'll introduce you to the team. Let me know if you need anything."

I smile and sit down.

My cubicle is plain and basic. I'll definitely need to fix that at some point. But there's a shiny new work laptop sitting there, and honestly, knowing I won't have to rely on my almost-deceased personal laptop fills me with unspeakable relief.

I secretly snap a picture of my setup to show Grandma later. I already know she's going to clutch her pearls when she sees this.

After about fifteen minutes, I head to the conference room. I'm the first to arrive. Slowly, more people file in. White men, white women, *white, white, white*. It's giving *snowstorm in June*. I'm not necessarily uncomfortable, since Brown was my first PWI bootcamp, but still, being the lone, cultured chocolate sunflower in a room like this is not my favorite experience.

Well, actually, I'm not completely alone. I casually notice one Black guy sitting near the back of the room. Good to know I'm not actually the only drop of chocolate in this establishment.

Ben introduces me to a few of my colleagues, Anna Russo and Lucas York, from the Corporate Events team.

Anna gives me a polite smile.

Lucas gives me a smile with something behind it. Something I can't quite put my finger on yet, but I already know I don't like it.

Ben starts the meeting, walking through deliverables and weekly priorities. After a few presentations, he returns to the front of the room.

"And today, we have a new team member joining us," he announces. "Amina Ali will be coming on board as a Junior Program Manager for Corporate Events. Amina, could you stand and introduce yourself?"

Oh God. Spotlight. Not what I need. All eyes are on me.

I stand, trying not to sway.

"Hello everyone," I say, projecting confidence I don't fully feel. "I'm Amina Ali. I'm excited to be joining the team and contributing to our projects."

I sit down quickly, before my knees rethink their commitment to holding me up.

After the meeting, a few people greet me casually, and the Black guy I noticed earlier walks over.

Tall. Warm skin. Strong jawline. Eyes that look like they actually pay attention. Hmm, he's cute.

"Hey, what's going on?" he says with an easy smile. "How's it going? I'm Donovan Davis, Senior Program Manager on the Executive Accounts Team."

I shake his hand. His grip is firm and steady.

"Nice to meet you, Donovan. I'm Amina."

"What team are you on again?" he asks.

"Corporate Events," I reply.

He nods. "Nice. That's what's up. Welcome to the team, madam. Let me know if you ever need anything, Miss lady."

There's something in his tone that feels so genuine and grounded. It stands out in a sea of corporate snowflakes. I hate to admit it, but it probably helps that he's kind of cute.

He walks away, and almost immediately, Lucas swoops in, like he's been waiting for his cue.

"So," Lucas says, "we're working on a couple of events with different requirements. Did you go to college?"

"Yes," I say. "I went to Brown for undergrad and then went to another school for grad school."

His eyebrows jump. "Oh. You went to Brown as in... Brown University? In New England?"

"Yes," I repeat, matching his energy with a sprinkle of sass. "That would be the one."

"Oh. That... makes sense."

I pause. "What do you mean, 'that makes sense?'"

"Well," he says casually, "you're just so articulate."

The air goes still.

There it is. The microaggression dressed up as a compliment.

The implication that my diction is surprising, exceptional, maybe even anomalous, for someone who looks like me.

I stare at him, every possible response forming and dissolving on my tongue.

Keep your composure, Mina.

He meant it as a compliment, I guess. But it wasn't. It was a reminder that even though I may be highly educated, I'm still Black.

Lucas walks away after his *articulate* comment, completely unaware that he's left a bruise he'll never see. I inhale slowly, exhale even slower, reminding myself that I cannot fuck this up. *Day one. Just get through day one, Amina.*

After the meeting disperses, people drift back to their offices and cubicles. I retreat to mine, trying to distract myself from the subtle bullshit by straightening the pens Ben gave me. Black, blue, red; also known as the corporate trinity. But my mind keeps replaying Lucas's voice like a broken record.

Articulate. So articulate.

As if eloquence is unexpected. As if my diction is some kind of anomaly.

I shake it off. I focus on my email account, HR forms, and setting up my workstation. I'm sure I'll have my work cut out for me at a place like this.

About an hour later, Anna appears at the edge of my cubicle with a bright, slightly nervous smile.

"Hey, Amina," she says, tucking a strand of hair behind her ear. "I was going downstairs to grab lunch, if you wanted to come?"

I pause, not really knowing what to say or think. This is unexpected, but it doesn't feel unwelcome. I appreciate the gesture, even if I'm still trying to decode her energy after the conversation I had with Lucas.

"Sure," I say, grabbing my bag. "Give me one second, Anna."

We walk to the café downstairs. It's very upscale. Minimalist décor and overpriced quinoa bowls. It seems like the kind of place that only gives you one salad dressing and then judges you silently if you ask for more.

We sit at a table toward the back, away from the crowd. Anna unwraps her sandwich neatly. I'm still deciding whether the sandwich looks like it belongs to a gerbil or human being. It appears to be nothing but tomatoes and greens, stacked between some sort of dry bread.

"So," she says cheerfully, "how's your first day going so far?"

"Not too bad," I say. "A bit overwhelming at times, but I'm excited to get the hang of things."

She nods enthusiastically. "That's totally normal. OHE can be a lot at first, but you'll adjust. We're all about culture here. Community. Collaboration."

The way she says *culture* makes me pause. I'm not sure where she's going with this yet.

"You know," she says, "I've been wondering... where does the name Amina come from?

I pause mid-chew and nearly choke on Grandma Jamila's baked barbecue mumbo chicken.

I'm shocked. Not because it's an offensive question by itself, but because of the way she asked it. As if my name is an artifact from a country she thinks I might have smuggled in my purse.

I blink. "Oh. Um... it's Arabic in origin."

"Ohhh," she says, dragging the vowel like she just solved a mystery, a murder trial, or some shit. "That makes sense. I knew it had to come from... from somewhere."

Somewhere.

These people here, I swear. As if somewhere does not include the United States. As if I, too, must have come from somewhere, that isn't the United States.

I swallow slowly. "Yep," I say reluctantly. "Just like names like Hannah, Elizabeth, or Rebecca come from somewhere."

I'm so petty.

Her eyes widen slightly. "Oh! No, I didn't mean it like that. I just meant... your name is very... unique."

Of course. Unique. The corporate synonym for *ethnic*.

I look back down at my food. "Right."

She takes a sip of her kombucha, then pivots the conversation.

"I'm really glad the company is taking diversity, equity, and inclusion seriously," she says, lowering her voice like she's saying something confidential.

I nearly choke on a grain of rice.

There it is.

Again...

The grenade. Casually tossed in my lap. I'm expected to cradle it, smile politely, and wait for it to explode.

She keeps talking, completely unaware that she has detonated anything.

"For a while, OHE was really... you know..." She gestures around the café as if the space itself explains her point. "But now, they're bringing in talent like you. It's a great step for morale."

Morale.

Not strategy.

Not capability.

Not skill.

Fucking Morale.

The fuck...

"Representation is important, I agree," I say carefully. "But I'm here because I'm qualified. I'm not a DEI hire."

Her eyes widen again. "Oh! Yes, of course. I didn't mean... obviously you're totally qualified. I just meant it's nice to see the company broadening its horizons."

I take a slow sip of my water to keep myself from responding prematurely and losing my job before the close of business.

When the silence finally dissipates, she slips back into her cheerfulness as if nothing happened.

"You're going to love it here. Corporate Events is like a family."

Yeah. A family where, apparently, I'm the diversity sculpture they decided to display in the lobby.

But I thank her anyway. It was kind of her to invite me to lunch, I guess, even if the conversation felt like I was only trying to prove myself to someone I have no obligation to prove myself to.

She takes the elevator up, and I decide to take the stairs to burn off my lunch. As I climb the stairwell, I replay the lunch in my head.

The name question. The diversity comment. The way she looked at me, as if I was an exciting new food she had heard of but never tasted, and finally got to try.

And yet... I breathe.

I remind myself that I belong here. In this building. In this moment. This is my opportunity to seize.

I push open the door to my floor, and the first person I see is Donovan Davis, standing a short distance down the hall near the copier. He glances up, catches my eye, and gives a nod. It's familiar and warm. It's how Black people acknowledge other Black people in public. He looks at me more intensely, like he's silently asking if I'm good.

And, for a brief second, I am. Looking at him gives me comfort. Maybe it's that familiarity that gives me comfort. I wonder if I'm wrong for finding comfort in a stranger. Either way, I am glad Donovan is here.

Maybe I can make this work. If Donovan made it work being the sole Black man, then I should be able to make it work too, being the sole Black woman. Even in this building full of polished glass and veiled assumptions. Even with people like Lucas and Anna assigning me narratives and stereotypes I never volunteered for.

Because I'm here, and this is just the beginning. Day one is almost over. Tomorrow, I keep it going.

4

Pressure Points

Two weeks in, and I've learned three things about OHE & Associates.

One, everyone drinks kombucha like it's holy water.

Two, no one actually knows how to use the copier, despite how nice it is, and how much they pretend otherwise. Everyone just kind of stands there and fiddles with it until it works.

And three, nothing reveals office politics faster than a high-visibility project, such as SPARK. Which is how I find myself sitting in Conference Room B at 9:07 a.m., staring at a slide titled:

SPARK

OHE & Associates' Flagship Corporate Experience Event

Big font with even bigger expectations.

Ben stands at the front of the room, remote in hand, and his posture is so relaxed. It's almost as if he's already survived the worst of corporate firestorms, so this doesn't faze him.

"SPARK is our biggest project of the year," he says, clicking to the next slide. "Clients fly in from everywhere. There will be press coverage, investors, and plenty of stakeholders in attendance. This is the event that sets the tone for the entire firm and helps bring in the funding and partnerships we need."

I glance at the agenda.

Theme.

Programming.

Experience Design.

Logistics.

Flow.

Translation: if this goes well, everyone wins. If it doesn't, I guess we all wonder whether or not we still have a job.

Ben turns to the Corporate Events Team.

"Amina, Anna, Lucas, you'll be leading the creative and programming side, meaning you all will be tasked to come up with a theme and plan the entire experience."

There it is. A little bit of responsibility.

Lucas straightens in his seat immediately, like he's been waiting for this moment his whole life. Anna smiles, tight but eager. I nod, calm on the outside, but mentally spiraling on the inside.

Two weeks in and I'm already assigned to the company's crown jewel. I don't know if I should be happy or panicking.

After the meeting, Lucas, Anna, and I find a table in the open workspace to start brainstorming. Laptops open, notebooks come out, and coffee cups are scattered between us like they're part of a setup. The coffee is already lukewarm, but we sip it anyway, tapping keys and jotting notes as we start tossing around ideas for SPARK.

"So," Anna says brightly, clapping once. "SPARK is all about innovation and momentum."

Lucas nods. "Yeah, it needs to feel... aspirational."

Aspirational is corporate for expensive but vague.

We pull up last year's SPARK deck from the archive. There were glass stages, LED walls, and a keynote speaker who looks like he says things like *lean in* without irony. The event seemed like it was polished and expensive, but from what I gather, it was more performative than memorable.

"What if," I say, a little tentative, "we focus less on glamour and more on authenticity?"

They both look at me.

"We're calling it SPARK," I continue. "So maybe it actually sparks something in people. Not just looks good in photos.

Anna nods. "I like that."

Lucas leans back in his chair. "Yeah, I mean, that is an idea. We'll see how it fits in with everything else."

Everything else being whatever he was already planning.

Eventually, the conversation fizzles out. Lucas is the first to disengage, like he's late for something important, when in reality, he isn't late for anything. Anna gathers her notes and gives me an encouraging smile.

"Let's sync later," she says. "See where we all land."

We'll see, I think.

I watch them walk off in opposite directions, then I open a blank document on my laptop. I don't start with speakers or schedules, because that will come later. I start with flow and feeling.

Arrival.

First impressions.

The subtle anxiety of walking into a room full of strangers.

The relief of feeling oriented.

The moments people lean into the conversation instead of scrolling on their phones.

SPARK, to me, is a story. A story about everything OHE & Associates has accomplished up to a point in time. Every good story has rhythm and a purpose. In this case, the purpose is to secure funding and partnerships. So we need to tell a story that is compelling enough to make people invest in us.

Hours pass without me noticing. By late afternoon, my eyes ache, and my coffee is cold, but my ideas still feel very much alive. This whole thing is exciting and reminds me of a group project in college.

Eventually, I decide it's quitting time. I shut my laptop, gather my things, and head out of the building. It's one of those nice days where the sun would be offended if I didn't give it a little extra FaceTime, so instead of going straight home, I decide to go look at apartments to keep me out the house for a little while longer.

I can't let work, exhaustion, or the excitement of being newly employed distract me from the other aspect of the goal. The job was never just about the job. It was supposed to lead me to a front door that's mine. If I'm going to survive work like this, I need a place that's made just for me.

As I walk toward the Metro, I scroll through listings on my phone, narrowing my search down to two apartments that look worthwhile for me to go see. I'm pretty set on staying in Amberline Heights for a multitude of reasons. One place is on the north side, the other on the south. Both are close enough that I would still be able to pull up on Grandma Jamila whenever I need real food, unsolicited advice, or both. I'm not ready to live so far away that a plate requires planning.

I arrive at the first apartment. It smells like cleaning supplies and ass. It also has an aggressive lemon scent that tries too hard to convince you that something bad didn't happen there recently. I don't stay long enough to investigate. I leave and continue my journey to the other apartment.

The second apartment is nice. Too nice. Floor-to-ceiling windows, stainless steel everything, and a rent price that is definitely too pricey for my pockets. I already know that I can't afford the place before the leasing agent finishes the tour. I continue the tour anyway, just to not completely waste our time. I smile politely and pretend I'm considering it.

By the time I step back outside, the conclusion is obvious. I'm going to have to stay with Grandma Jamila a little longer, even though I'm working. I think it'll be best to save up a few more checks and really take my time finding a place.

Not because I can't completely afford to move, but because I refuse to rush into something, and potentially end up with something I don't actually want or like. I don't need a luxury place, but I do need a pretty nice place if I'm being honest. If I'm going to step out on my own, it has to feel intentional. Like a step forward, not just away.

Grandma Jamila won't mind. She'll act like she does, complain a little, talk her shit, and ask way too many questions about my job and my life. But she'll want me there. She always does. And honestly, staying a little longer makes sense. I probably should let the checks stack before I change my address and act all brand new.

***

The next morning, I'm back at work early, coffee in hand, already in my notes before most people have even logged on. I'm still riding the momentum from the meeting, eager to keep pushing on the SPARK ideas while they're still fresh in my mind. That's when a shadow pauses at the edge of my cubicle.

"How's SPARK treating you?"

I look up. It's Donovan, leaning casually against the edge of my cubicle. He has no jacket on. His sleeves are rolled up just enough to show his forearm definition, which suggests that he probably knows his way around somebody's gym.

"Busy," I say. "In a good way."

He nods, glancing at the screen, then back at me." That project has a way of revealing what people are really made of."

I raise an eyebrow in curiosity. "Is that a warning?"

He smiles. "More like an observation, ma'am."

He doesn't linger. Just taps the edge of my desk once and moves on, leaving behind the faint sense that he clocked more than he said.

***

The rest of the week blurs together. I move through it on autopilot, even though it still requires my full attention. I come in early, leave a little later than I mean to, and spend most days toggling between focus and finessing it. I'm doing my best, trying to put in extra effort when I can.

Every day, I try a different coffee, because apparently, the corporate world runs on coffee and meetings. The barista knows my name now, and that feels like a corporate milestone. I've officially reached a new level of corporate baddie.

I end up spending more time with Anna and Lucas than I expect to, which gives me a front-row seat to their personalities. Lucas likes an audience. His voice carries across the office, confident and performative, as if everything he says deserves a standing ovation. He's so fucking full of himself. Anna is different, though. She seems more genuine. I watch her as her desk slowly fills with color swatches and printed concepts for SPARK.

I keep my head down and my hands busy. Not because I'm disengaged, but because I'm locked in. I'm watching, listening, and editing my own ideas down to the sharpest version. I know, there is no room for error on my part.

I start building my SPARK concept the way I understand things best, like a story. An opening with tension and momentum. A middle that pulls people in, instead of letting them drift away. Moments designed to hold attention, not just ones that look good in photos and on social media. By the end of the week, it's finally starting to feel like it's something real and something feasible.

By Friday night, I'm back at Grandma Jamila's, stretched out on my bed, notes scattered everywhere like I'm mapping out a crime scene I refuse to abandon.

The work week is finally over, but SPARK lives on the screen in front of me, half-built and already demanding more of my attention than I'd like. My mind is still running with ideas and thoughts. I want everything to be perfect.

I lean back against the headboard and close my eyes for a second, reminding myself that I survived the week. My body is done; however, my mind did not get the memo. So many thoughts enter my mind.

Finally, somewhere between ideas and other thoughts, I find the quiet again. I can hear the world around me again. I hear the old rowhouse settling. My thoughts finally slow down enough to hear my own heartbeat in my ear.

I stretch my arms above my head, my shirt riding up just enough the let the cool air kiss my skin. The cold air grounds me. It pulls me back into my body like it was saving me from myself. Sometimes our thoughts and our minds can be our own worst enemies.

For a second, everything is calm. But then, my mind drifts back to earlier in the week. Back to the little pit stop Donovan made at my desk. He wasn't there long, but he was there long enough to leave an impression, at least on me.

The way his eyes flashed to my screen, then back to me. The way his voice dropped when he spoke. The way he didn't say more than he needed to.

He was professional and controlled, still, I wonder what actually made him stop by my desk. I haven't seen him do that with anyone else. Maybe it's because we're both Black, navigating a similar experience at OHE & Associates. Maybe he thinks I'm pretty. Then again, maybe I'm reading into it too much. Either way, I can't deny that the man is fine, and my brain refuses to ignore that particular fact.

I stare up at the ceiling, letting the thought marinate in my mind. I tell myself it's nothing, but I'm struggling to get the thought of Donovan out of my head. Maybe it's hormones. Maybe it's delusion, or maybe it's the unfamiliar feeling of being seen.

I exhale and roll onto my side.

It's Friday... The workweek is officially over, and I refuse to donate my weekend to a man I barely know or a project that will still be there when I return to work. Donovan can wait. SPARK can definitely wait. The weekend belongs to me.

I reach for the remote and turn on one of my comfort shows, and watch other people's chaos, to distract me from my own. All I need now is a cozy throw blanket, something salty, something sweet, and the permission to just be a woman at rest. There will be plenty of time to be sharp, ambitious, and curious.

But tonight, I let the week end.

5

Donovan

It has been over a month since I started at OHE & Associates, and the novelty has officially worn off. The Corporate Events team feels tighter now, not closer, just compressed, like everyone is holding their breath while working on SPARK. The pressure is everywhere, in emails, in meetings that run long without saying much, in the way people talk around ideas instead of to them. I've learned where I fit in the room, which is somewhere between visible and invisible. I'm trusted just enough to carry weight but still questioned enough to remind me that I'm new here. The microaggressions haven't stopped, they've just gotten quieter and a little more polished. They're always wrapped in smiles and corporate jargon. Somehow, that makes them harder to call out and easier to internalize.

My mind has been wrapped around SPARK. I keep asking myself how much effort I should put into this, being that I'm the new kid on the block. Anna and Lucas have been here for years. They know the angles, the unspoken rules, the politics. And me... I'm still trying to figure shit out, like why my badge never scans on the first try.

It's exhausting, the way this place drains me, sometimes. Not because I dislike the work, though. The work itself is actually pretty interesting. It's the people here that drain me most. The way they look at me. The way they underestimate me. I literally went to Brown. I got in based on merit, not because someone needed to fill a quota. But the way some of the folks here treat me, you would think I barely graduated from community college.

At home, though, it is a different story. Grandma Jamila keeps telling me to stay at OHE & Associates for at least a year. She thinks longevity looks good on a résumé. Grandma comes from the era where once you got a job, you stayed until they handed you a retirement cake and a pat on the back. She means well, but she also worked the same job for forty years. You got me completely messed up if you think I am staying at OHE for four decades.

At least now, I know why people praise Fridays and hump days so much. Because sitting on this nasty ass train every morning to go somewhere I cannot fully be myself at is... an experience I'll say. Even though this job was an answered prayer, sometimes it feels like a test that will not end.

But there is one thing I genuinely look forward to at OHE and Associates.

Donovan.

Donovan Davis.

Mr. Davis, if we're being formal.

Senior Program Manager for the Executive Accounts Team. A Morehouse man. A D9 fraternity man. Smooth in that very subtle, very dangerous way that is only found at HBCUs and in the pages of romance novels and bottles of expensive red wine.

He is brilliant. Accomplished. Award-winning. And... the only Black man in this entire office. The way he carries himself in meetings is almost regal. He speaks with ease, like language was designed for him. He commands a room without forcing anything. I watch him sometimes and wonder how he learned to carry himself like that. Maybe he could teach me.

And Lord, the man smells good. I don't know if he bathes in shea butter and heaven, but whenever he passes me, I consider writing a thank you letter to whoever created his cologne.

Not to mention the body. The way his shirts hug his chest and arms... oh my. There are biceps and triceps that I didn't even know existed until Donovan walked past my cubicle one Tuesday morning.

Whenever he speaks to me, I get nervous in the most embarrassing way. Words disappear, and my brain stutters. My heart tries to audition for a drumline every time I see him. In staff meetings, I often catch him looking at me. Not in a creepy way, and he isn't being inappropriate. Just... present maybe. I can tell he's curious about me, but I don't know why. And when I look back, he always looks away, like he doesn't want me to see whatever it is that he's feeling.

He is a breath of fresh air in a building full of white fog. The thought of him makes it that much easier clocking into work. I always look forward to seeing a fine man.

I walk into the office and greet the receptionist, Stacy. She always wears bright lipstick and a smile that is somehow both friendly and suspicious.

"Good morning, Amina," she says.

"Good morning, Stacy."

I hurry to my cubicle to check my email before the staff meeting. Then like clockwork, I head to the conference room for the staff meeting when it's time.

When the meeting starts, Ben jumps right in.

"Our December SPARK event is twelve weeks away. This event is critical, as it kicks off our engagements for Q1 of the next year. We need perfection."

Everyone nods like we all just enlisted in the military or some shit.

"All junior program managers will be paired with a senior PM for specific deliverables," he continues. "Check your email for assignments."

The meeting ends, and everyone scatters back to their offices. I head back to my cubicle to check my email to see who I am paired with. I get back to my desk, open my laptop, but before I can even open my email, there is a soft knock on the side of my cubicle.

It's Donovan.

I'm unsure what he is doing here at my cubicle again. This man can't seem to stay away from me, or maybe that's just my wishful thinking.

He leans against the cubicle wall, his smile calm and... something else. Something that makes heat crawl up my neck and butterflies fly in my stomach.

"Hey," he says. "Looks like we are paired together."

I look up at him and freeze like a deer in headlights.

"We are...?" My voice cracks a little.

Donovan laughs quietly, "Cheer up, buttercup. You are treating me like I have the cooties."

I shake my head fast, "No, no, no. Not at all. I am happy we get the opportunity to work together. You are revered around here, and I'm sure there's a lot I can learn from you."

"Good," he says. "Let's talk through the project over lunch. Meet me in the café at 12:15."

"Okay," I say.

He taps the cubicle wall lightly. "See you then, Miss Ali." His laugh is low, warm, and entirely too damn sexy.

He walks away, and I blink at my computer screen. Why would they pair me with him? How am I supposed to focus when I can smell him from ten feet away? How am I supposed to think about work without thinking about how fine that man is?

Get it together, Mina.

I force myself to work and stay busy until 12:10, then head to lunch. When I walk into the café, I see Donovan immediately. You can't miss a six-foot, caramel-complexioned Black man in a building full of people named Brad.

"Mr. Davis", I say as I approach the table.

He stands up and pulls out my chair.

Oh. He is a gentleman too...

"Ms. Ali," he says with a smile.

We sit, and for a moment the air between us feels almost... thick. Not awkward, just thick. More like unspoken possibilities. I pull my water bottle out of my lunchbox and take a sip because my mouth has become so parched in this thick air.

"So," he says, "what did you bring for lunch?"

"Coconut Curry Shrimp," I say. "One of my favorite comfort meals. What about you?"

He lifts a slice of pizza. "I am a bachelor, if you didn't know. I don't know how to cook very well, so I eat out pretty often."

I laugh quietly. "So, you are single." I try to hide the fact that this is the real information I wanted; I could care less about the pizza.

He smiles but doesn't elaborate further.

To distract myself from the thought of how good he looks, I talk about my concept for SPARK. "Since this year marks the twentieth anniversary of SPARK, I suggest including a timeline that highlights the company's most successful projects over the years."

"I love that," he says. "Send me your draft when you're ready."

"Will do," I say.

"So," he adds casually, "you went to Brown. How was it?"

"It was amazing. Cold. Brutally cold. But intellectually, it was the most stimulating experience I have ever had." I tilt my head. "What about Morehouse?"

"It shaped me," he says, simply. "In every way. I'm grateful to have been able to have an amazing HBCU experience at one of the most respected schools and graduate from the top of my class."

Something about what he says makes my heart fold into itself and respect him that much more. He's fine and educated, hmm, shout out to whoever raised him.

"So," he asks, "do you have a family?"

I wonder if he is trying to see if anyone is waiting for me at home.

"It is just me," I say. "I live in Amberline Heights with my grandmother, for now, until I get my apartment."

His eyebrows lift, and his mouth opens. "I live there too. Well, in Amberline Heights."

"What? No way."

He nods. "Small world."

We lock eyes without meaning to, and we stay locked there for a moment. He looks at me, and I look at him. Neither of us look away immediately. Five seconds feels like a lifetime. I wonder what he's thinking. I wonder if he's wondering what I'm thinking.

I clear my throat. "Well, we should probably, you know, head back to work."

"Of course," he says. "Let me toss my trash."

We walk separately, but the space between us feels charged. I make it back to my desk, turn my laptop on, and get back to work.

Ping.

A message pops up on my screen. It's an instant message from Donovan.

Donovan Davis:

Thanks for having lunch with me.

Amina Ali:

You're welcome.

Donovan Davis:

Your concept is great. We just need to make sure it's better than what Lucas and Anna come up with.

Amina Ali:

I mean, is it really that serious?

Donovan Davis:

Yes, it is. What Ben did not tell you is that you can get a bonus for this. Plus, you have been here less than a year, so it'll be impressive to get credit for this so early on in your career here.

Amina Ali:

Well, in that case, yes, I want to do the best I can, because I sure could use a bonus.

Donovan Davis:

Good. That is what I like to hear. Same time tomorrow. Lunch?

Amina Ali:

Yes.

Donovan Davis:

:)

I stare at the little smiley face, shocked at how well I handled that. Did we just schedule a date? Okay, maybe it's just a professional lunch meeting. At least, that is what we are calling it at this juncture.

But it feels like a date to me.

***

The next day.

It's 11:30, and I can't focus at all. All I can think about is Donovan. His laugh. His eyes. The moment we held each other's gaze like two people trying to read a book written only for them. I just want to see him again. I think I'm... I'm... infatuated.

At 12:10, I head to the café. Once I get there, I quickly realize Donovan is not in the café. I hear my name being called from behind me, and I look and see Donovan waiting by the door, so I walk to him.

"Amina," he says softly. "How are you?"

"I am well," I say, feeling suddenly shy. "Are we not eating here?"

"There's this ramen spot I want to try," he says. "My treat. It is a nice day. We should change the scenery."

I oblige. "I'm down, lead the way."

We walk ten minutes or so away from the office. I watch his stride, confident and relaxed. He looks like a man who knows where he is going. I'm guessing he does, because as I'm thinking that we're arriving at a swanky ramen spot.

Once we walk in, I scope the scene. It's nice and quaint. It's not quite a restaurant per se, it's a place where you order the food at a cashier, and then you are free to sit down and eat. I order Teriyaki Udon noodles with shrimp. He orders spicy Dan Dan noodles. Once we grab the food, we find a table and sit down, and chat while we eat.

"So," I say, "you must come here all the time."

He shakes his head. "Nope. Never been here before. I thought it would be nice to try it together."

Did he just say together?

My heart flutters.

"That was thoughtful," I say.

He smirks. "I try."

I steer the conversation toward work, telling him how my research is coming along, but he doesn't seem too interested in hearing about that.

"Well, Miss Ali," he says playfully, "I am happy to hear that."

He takes a large bite of noodles, then adds, "There's one subject I 'm interested in researching myself."

I look at him with nothing but curiosity. "What subject would that be, Mr. Davis?"

"You," he says.

I almost choke. "Me?"

"Yes," he answers. "We are colleagues, but we're the only two Black people in that building, and we live in the same neighborhood. I would like to get to know you a little better. And... it doesn't hurt that you give me something nice to look at during the workday."

We both erupt in laughter.

"So, what do you want to know?" I ask.

"Not today," he says. "First, I need to get you out of those clothes."

I choke again. "Excuse me?"

He raises his hands. "Not like that. I meant something more comfortable. You ran track, right? How about we go jogging this weekend? Then I will take you to breakfast."

My heart is pounding so loud, it feels like everyone can see it.

"Well," I say, "I hope you stretched, because you are about to get smoked."

He laughs. "That was hella corny."

We finish lunch and walk back to the office. Once we get there, we split ways as if nothing ever happened. Like we didn't just plan a date.

I keep asking myself what is happening between us. Whatever it is, it doesn't feel accidental. It definitely feels like something more than merely being professional.

I am not naïve. I know where I work. I know the rules, written and unwritten. I'm not trying to cross professional lines or create problems in a place where I'm still trying to find my footing. Still, curiosity has a way of slipping past good sense. I find myself wondering who Donovan Davis is outside of conference rooms and OHE & Associates. Just as he wants to know more about me, I want to know more about him, and I can't deny that.

I've always had a way of playing with fire. This little cat and mouse game that we're playing makes me feel something close to excitement. I'm not saying that Donovan Davis is the beginning of anything. I'm not saying that he and I will be anything. I'm saying he feels like a breath of fresh air.

And with him, I might finally start breathing again.

6

The Watching

I've been at OHE & Associates for two months now, and... interesting is the only word that describes how I feel about the place.

Not good. Not bad. Just... interesting. Like a show you're not sure you like yet, but you keep watching because something is telling you a plot twist is coming. You're holding on to hope that things may actually get better.

I know the layout of the office now. I know which floors smell like coffee and which smell like copier ink and regret. I know who microwaves fish and who runs their meetings like hostage negotiations. Hell, I even know who uses the bathroom and doesn't wash their hands. Which reminds me, I've got to stop shaking people's hands.

But knowing the layout isn't the same as belonging. And for some reason, despite working hard, speaking eloquently, and showing up prepared every day, the feeling of belonging hasn't reached me yet. I still feel like an outsider.

I've been deep in my research and planning for the SPARK presentation. It's quite fascinating to see that OHE has been involved in everything from real estate projects to major fashion events. They've had their hands in industries I didn't even know intersected with the corporate world. It's quite impressive, and little ole me gets to be involved in all of it. Yeah, it's cool, I guess. But some days I still feel like a visiting student on a field trip.

Corporate politics? I'm learning...

The Corporate Events Team is tolerable. Anna has grown on me, despite our conversation in the café a while back. She's smart and witty. I respect it.

Lucas, though...

Something about him feels off. It's like he masks envy with fake friendliness. He compliments me with one breath and doubts me with the next. In my opinion, he's a hater.

But today is another team meeting day with Ben, so I'm putting on my best professional poise face. Regardless of how I feel, I'm still going to show up every day, and I'm still going to do my part. I always keep the fact that all bets are on me in the back of my head.

I gracefully open the conference room door.

"Hey team," I say, walking in like I own the place. Which I don't, but my stilettos do. They click across the floor with authority. Today's look? I ate down.

Both Anna and Lucas glance up and smile. Maybe at me. Maybe at the outfit. Either way, they notice me.

Moments later, Ben walks in, bright and cheerful like he's fueled entirely by optimism and cheap caffeine.

"My favorite Corporate Events Team! How's everyone doing?" he says, clapping his hands.

We all murmur variations of "good," "great," and "hanging in there," like a choir of corporate sopranos and altos.

"So," Ben continues, "for SPARK, I know each of you is working on your individual concepts and capabilities decks, but I forgot to mention one thing..."

He pauses dramatically.

"We're only moving forward with one idea this year, rather than combining all of them."

We all look at each other with confusion. I genuinely thought each of our concepts would be used in some type of way.

Ben nods. "Yes, only one. You'll each present to me, Tony, and some other key management personnel. We'll choose whichever concept fits the vision. No pressure."

He smiles like he didn't just set us up for the *Corporate Hunger Games*. I guess Donovan was right, I really do need to beat Anna and Lucas.

After the meeting, Anna and Lucas leave together, chatting like they typically do. I gather my laptop and binder, and my phone vibrates. It's a text from Grandma Jamila.

Did you eat lunch, Mina? Or you up there fainting in that building?

I smile and text back.

I'm good, Grandma. I had a snack.

She's always so concerned about me, and even as a grown woman, I still appreciate her for the way she shows me so much love. I can only hope to one day be able to repay her for all she has done for my siblings and me.

As I head toward my cubicle, something catches my eye. My workstation light is on. I know for a fact that I turned it off.

I always turn it off.

I slow down, and once I get closer, I see...

Lucas is sitting at my desk.

Not near my desk. Not walking by my desk. Sitting. In my chair, looking through my notes and research. What the fuck is he doing?

"Lucas," I say calmly, "can I help you with something?"

I must have startled him, because he jumped up as if a mouse ran out.

"Amina, Hey. Yes, I was, uh... just checking on something."

"In my notes?" I ask, with a little bit of attitude.

He scratches the back of his neck like he's trying to rub out a lie. "Well, you weren't here yet, and I needed the updated metrics we discussed earlier. I thought maybe you'd written them down in your notes."

"I didn't," I say sternly. "But even if I did, checking my personal notes isn't appropriate and it's a major breach of professional boundaries."

My tone is polite, but my diction is surgical. That's when he realizes he's not dealing with a fool.

"I wasn't snooping," he blurts out, which is exactly what someone says when they've been caught snooping.

I take a step closer. Not confrontational, but just enough so he feels my energy.

"I would appreciate," I say, articulating each word clearly, "if in the future, you ask me directly for whatever it is that you need. I'm happy to collaborate, but access to my workstation is not part of that arrangement."

Lucas' expression shifts. His embarrassment warps into defensiveness.

"You do not need to catch an attitude," he says quietly, as if he is the reasonable one.

I blink slowly.

"An attitude," I repeat. "Interesting choice of words."

He shrugs. "I'm just saying... it isn't that serious."

I tilt my head like a puppy. "So, when a Black woman sets a boundary, suddenly it is an attitude. That seems very serious to me."

His mouth opens, but no words come out. A flush rises up his neck. At this point, his face is as red as a cherry.

"I was not implying that," he mumbles.

"You implied enough," I say softly. "How about this... we can both do better moving forward, and we can both agree to not intrude on each other's workstations."

I hold his gaze for an extra couple of seconds, just long enough for him to understand I did not come here timid or unaware. He looks down and backs away, mumbling something under his breath that sounds like an apology; however, he lacks the courage to fully materialize it.

When he finally leaves, I sit and breathe, trying desperately to control myself and my emotions. If it's one thing I hate, it's people touching my shit. I open my notes and skim through them. Everything looks untouched, but the message is clear. He was not curious. He was calculating. He was definitely snooping, I'm convinced.

I just know he wanted to see my research. He wanted to know what angle I was taking for SPARK. It's funny because he was so sure that we would only consider my ideas, but as soon as Ben says that this has basically turned into a competition, he suddenly wants to see what I've come up with.

I lean back in my chair and whisper to myself, "All right then. If we are playing this game, let's play it correctly."

I may be new. I may be young. I may be the only Black woman in this piece, but... I did not survive Brown, grad school, and life in the hood by being naïve.

I'm still sitting at my desk, organizing my notes, still replaying the confrontation with Lucas in my head. I think I handled it rather well. I was a complete professional. But the sting of it, the aftertaste of it, is still sitting in my chest like gravity.

My phone vibrates beside my keyboard.

Meet me at the Amberline Heights Rec Center this Saturday at 9 a.m. Wear something you can run in.

I stare at the message.

I know exactly who it is, but the question is, how did he even get my number? It has to be him. Nobody else in my life would be bold enough to text me, demanding that I do something. That screams confidence, and Donovan is just that. It's like he already knows I'll show up. I mean, I did agree to come, but still...

I type back quickly.

Who is this?

A few minutes pass, then a response.

I thought my number would have been saved by now. Disappointed, Miss Ali.

A smile creeps across my face before I can stop it. Here come the butterflies again. They always come when he talks to me.

I didn't know we were close enough for saved contact status. I don't even know how you got my number, but I guess I'll save yours.

We are getting there. Saturday. 9 a.m.

I bite my lip. The audacity. The confidence... The way he does not ask, he tells. He just created the space for me to step into, and I'm stepping.

I'll be there.

Very good.

I lock my phone and lean back in my office chair, staring at the ceiling like it might explain what is happening to me.

This is a man I should keep a professional distance from. A man who works where I work. A man who sees everything, hears everything, and reads me in a way that makes me feel more exposed than I care to admit.

But despite all of that...

Something about him feels familiar, and he feels safe. He feels like someone who knows how heavy it is to walk into rooms alone and still hold your head high.

And the truth is, I want to see him.

Not just as a coworker. Not just as another Black professional trying to survive corporate America.

I want to see *him.*

7

A Good Morning

I wake up at 7:30 in the morning on Saturday. The sun is shining and the birds are chirping. That's typically the start to a great day.

"It's Saturdaaaaay," I scream out, with every bit of excitement in my soul.

"Amina, what in the hell are you screaming for this early in the morning?" Grandma Jamila yells back like she's got beef with happiness itself.

I walk into the kitchen where she's sitting at the table, drinking her morning coffee with that nasty ass powdered creamer she swears by. The woman refuses to buy real creamer because she claims it spoils too fast. *Whatever.*

"I'm just happy," I say, cheesing like I'm in a dental office commercial.

She eyes me suspiciously over her mug. "You better not be having sex in my house, woman."

"Grandma... ain't nobody having sex," I say while tying my tennis shoes.

"Where you going this early?" she asks.

"I'm going jogging."

"Mmhmm. She squints at my leggings. "With them tight ass pants, you must be going jogging for sex."

"Grandma, please. Enough about sex. I'm literally going running with a colleague. Relax." I kiss her cheek. "Be blessed, ma'am."

I hurry outside to the bus stop before she can start interrogating me about birth control and all the other shit she can come up with.

Once I get to the bus stop, I just stand there and wait for the bus to pull up. It's quiet today, just me and an older gentleman waiting. The bus pulls up after five minutes, and I hop on and take the short ride to Amberline Heights Recreation Center.

By the time I get there, it's only 8:30 a.m. I scroll on my phone, expecting to wait a while since I arrived so early, but five minutes later, I hear loud bass vibrating through the parking lot. A tinted-out black Tahoe pulls up, Kendrick Lamar blasting through the speakers.

Damn. That's my song.

I do a little two-step in place; nothing crazy. I'm waiting to see which around-the-way dude is about to hop out.

The music cuts off, and the door swings open. To my surprise, Donovan steps out. I swear my soul momentarily leaves my body.

He looks like he just stepped out of God's personal gym, like the Lord himself had a hand in the sculpting of his body and then stood back to admire his work. The white compression athletic tank clings to him shamelessly, outlining every earned curve of muscle. My eyes drift, doing a slow, disrespectful inventory of his body, and I realize I can count at least six tattoos from where I'm standing. There may be more hiding under the fabric, which feels unfair, but also intriguing. He has on hoochie daddy shorts that make me consider being a hoochie for him today. They look so good on him, they might make me consider throwing my own decorum in the trash and being his problem for now. Just for today, though. Just for him.

At work, Donovan is always clean-cut and polished. Out here, though, he looks different. He's still composed, but clearly, this is the version of him that HR never gets to meet. Raw in a way that feels unfiltered. Sexy in a way that sneaks up on you. Delicious in that dangerous, slow-burn way, like a meal you were not planning on craving but suddenly cannot stop thinking about.

He jogs over and pulls me into a quick half-hug, like the kind you give people in church. My body betrays me immediately, tingling from the contact like it's been waiting all morning for this exact moment. I won't complain, though.

"What's up, Amina," he says, smiling like he's been waiting this whole time. "You look nice."

I fight the urge to melt into a puddle right on the pavement. "You don't look too bad yourself, Mr. Davis," I say, doing my best to sound composed and not like I mentally counted how many days a week he lifts.

He laughs. "Come on, track star. Let's hit the pavement."

We walk through the rec center and back out toward the track, easing into a jog side by side. The morning air is crisp, with just enough pollution and grit to remind you exactly where you are. The sun is gentle, not demanding anything yet other than me, my breath, and the rhythm of our steps.

"So," I say after a few laps, unable to help myself, "you like Kendrick?"

The question slips out with a grin, mostly because the sight of Donovan stepping out of that Tahoe with Kendrick blasting still hasn't fully processed in my mind, and I need him to confirm that it really happened.

Donovan laughs, a warm sound that sits deep in his chest. "Yeah, he is definitely in my top ten favorite rappers list," he says.

"Really?" I look over at him. "You know, at work, you don't strike me as the Kendrick type. I gesture at the hoochie daddy shorts, the tattoos, the tank top clinging to every muscle like it's committed to the cause. "But seeing you like this... it's different."

He smirks, eyes catching mine in a very flirtatious manner.

"At work, I play the game," he says. "But when I'm home in Amberline Heights, this is who I am."

Him saying that makes the moment so much better. I appreciate an authentic man, especially when he's proud of where he's from. So, it all hits me. Not in a romantic way, although yes, that too, but in a real, genuine way. Like he's letting me see the part of himself that doesn't come with a title or a dress code. I feel honored that he's willing to share this space with me.

Amberline Heights Donovan is down to earth in a way I can resonate with. He's not flashy or doing too much, just easy, like someone I could have grown up knowing. The kind of man who feels like a homie first, the type you would see posted on the block or leaning against a car, laughing at random shit. He is a little hood, that is clear. There is definitely a shared understanding. Of course, he is fine, and I know other women notice too.

Work Donovan is polished and strategic, corporate-perfect down to the posture and the pauses. He knows when to speak, when to listen, and when to keep his hands folded just right. Watching those two versions exist in the same body, right in front of me, does something to me. It feels intimate, like being invited into a part of him most people never get to see. The part that comes before the code-switch and after the armor.

We run a few more steps, quietly absorbing the moment. The sun is rising behind the rec center, spilling soft gold across the track and catching on his toasted caramel skin. He looks like something pulled straight out of an art gallery, all strong lines and restraint, beauty that does not beg to be noticed but still gets its way. The hint of a five o'clock shadow only contributes to his sexiness.

I clear my throat, mostly to remind myself that I have one. "So," I ask, keeping my tone light, "which Donovan am I running with right now?"

He glances down at me, a small smile playing at the corner of his mouth. "A mix," he says. "But mostly the real one."

Interesting.

We keep jogging, and I can feel him relaxing even more, showing pieces of himself that never appear in the aesthetically pleasing walls of OHE & Associates.

"You know," he says, growing up around here teaches you how to move and navigate two opposing worlds. In Amberline Heights, you have to be real and sometimes hard. At OHE, you have to be strategic, especially if you look like us." He lets out a quiet breath. "I learned early that code switching wasn't optional for success. Instead, it's a requirement to be successful if you're Black."

I nod in agreement, because I feel that on a deeper level. "That's exactly how I feel," I say. "Like I'm always translating myself. Switching how I talk, how I move, how much of me I let show. Switching everything."

He slows slightly, not enough to stop us, but just enough that we're literally touching.

"The trick," he says quietly, "is making sure to know who you are underneath all that."

That... resonates.

We settle into a steady rhythm, the sound of our shoes hitting the track creating a rhythm that is similar to a heartbeat. The tension between us feels anticipatory, not rushed or overwhelming. It's just present, and undeniably there.

After another lap, Donovan smiles over at me. "Alright, Brown University," he says. Let's see what you really got, ma."

I laugh. "Don't play with me, Morehouse."

He takes off without warning, sprinting down the straightaway like he has something to prove. I go right after him. The wind slaps my face, my legs wake up, and muscle memory slides in like it never left. For a few seconds, we are neck and neck, where I could just feel his presence without even looking at him.

Then I pass him. With ease...

He tries to catch up, but I leave him just far enough behind to bruise his ego just a little. When I slow down at the end of the straightaway, he jogs up laughing, hands on his hips, breath coming quick.

"Oh, nah," he says, shaking his head. "You really smoked me. "Okay, track star."

"You challenged me," I reply, smiling. "I just followed instructions. Your instructions might I add."

He laughs again, and his eyes are still locked on me. "That is wild. At work, you're all soft-spoken and professional. Out here, you talking trash."

I shrug. "I'm multifaceted."

"That you are," he says, looking at me as if I'm some type of dessert he wants to devour.

The air thickens between us again. It is so fucking charged. Like lightning deciding if it wants to strike.

We walk a cool-down lap. This time our arms brush once, then again. Neither of us pulls away.

"So," he says, casual but curious, "you asked me if I like Kendrick. What about you? Who's on your playlist?"

"A little bit of everything, I say. "Neo-soul for when I want to feel happy and grown. Afrobeats when I need joy. Rap when I need to remember who I am."

Donovan looks at me in a way that feels less like flirting and more like he's actually listening. Still spicy, though.

"So, who are you then? He asks.

I pause and think before I answer. I take a breath, looking ahead at the track stretching out in front of us.

"I'm a woman on a mission," I say finally. "I'm trying to break generational curses for my family. Trying to build something different than what I grew up with. Something stable. Something that lasts for generations to come."

I glance at him. "I want my future kids to have choices. Options. I want them to know that life can be bigger than just survival."

He nods slowly, impressed. "That's real," he says. "I fuck with it."

"And beyond that," I add, exhaling, letting the honesty come out clean, "I'm trying to figure out who I am without everybody else's expectations glued to me."

Donovan looks at me with something that feels like recognition. It's almost as if he knows exactly how that feels.

"I resonate with that, Amina."

Something in my spirit loosens when he speaks to me. I don't know why it hits me like that, but it does. The way he looks at me feels intentional without feeling invasive, like he's paying attention instead of inspecting and critiquing me. There's a difference, and I feel it.

We continue walking silently for a moment, letting our words sit between us. The air shifts, subtle but undeniable, almost like the moment right before a storm decides whether it's actually coming.

Then Donovan bumps me with his shoulder slightly. "You know," he says, you say all that like you're not already doing it."

I look up at him, confused. "Doing what?"

"Breaking curses. Changing the narrative. Showing up for yourself even when people make it harder than it needs to be." He looks at me then, really looks. "You think I haven't noticed?"

That catches me off guard. I don't respond immediately, and he doesn't push.

"I get it," he finally says. "Being the only one navigating a place not built for you. Trying to stay authentic without giving anyone a reason to question your worth. It's a balancing act."

I nod. "Yeah. Some days it feels like I'm walking a tightrope."

"Yeah, and some days," he says, "you're building the damn rope while walking it."

I laugh because it's too accurate. "Exactly."

We head inside the recreation center, into the basketball court. A group of older men are playing pick-up basketball, yelling across the court, talking shit like they're trying to win a championship. The sound feels like home. Amberline Heights is loud and cultured in the best way. Our way.

Donovan watches the game for a second, then looks back at me. "This is why I come here," he says. "This is my reset. Work will try to turn you into something you're not. Out here, nobody gives a damn who you are at OHE & Associates. You just exist."

"I really needed this," I admit, quieter than I mean to be.

He bumps my shoulder, like he understands exactly what I'm saying without me having to explain it further.

We make our way to the bleachers and stretch for a moment. The quiet hangs between us again, but not in an awkward way. Instead, it's comfortable. Our bodies are cooling down, but I can't lie, something else seems to be heating up.

"So," he says with a smirk, "you smoked me earlier. I think I definitely owe you a winner's breakfast."

A smile slides across my lips before I can stop it, and now all my teeth are exposed.

"Well," I say, dragging the word just a little, "I am not opposed to breakfast. I sure am hungry."

He laughs hysterically. "Why do you sound like the main character in *The Color Purple* right now?" He shakes his head, clearly amused. "Say less, I'll drive."p

***

We walk out of the recreation center, side by side. When we reach the parking lot, that black Tahoe is sitting there like it owns the lot. His Tahoe has tinted windows. black rims, which are a subtle flex. This is one of those vehicles that makes you think twice about fucking with the driver.

He opens the passenger door for me, and I climb inside. The seat is still warm from the sun. Before he even gets in on his side, the speakers come alive.

Kendrick Lamar.

The same song from earlier.

Kendrick's verses spill through the speakers, sharp and confident, every bar landing just right. For a second, the car feels less like a vehicle and more like a vibe, almost as if I accidentally stepped into Club Donovan and forgot what time it was.

Donovan settles into the driver's seat, glances over at me with a look I'm not quite ready to decode. We sit there in silence, letting the beat sink into our souls.

About ten minutes later, we pull up to this hole-in-the-wall spot in the cut, tucked between a liquor store and a nail salon. The sign outside is slightly crooked, one of the letters flickering, as if it gave up years ago. From the outside, it looks questionable. It's without a doubt the kind of place you would absolutely judge if you didn't know any better.

I glance at Donovan. "You sure about this?"

He laughs as he parks the Tahoe. "Trust me, woman, this is the best breakfast around here."

"Alright then, I'm going to take your word this time."

He laughs and steps out and walks around to open my door. "You can't let aesthetics fool you," he says. "Some of the best things don't look like much at first."

When he says it, it feels like he's referring to more than breakfast.

The second we walk inside, the smell wraps around me and holds me hostage. Butter, syrup, coffee. This is the type of smell that makes your stomach growl on instinct. The place is small, but it's jumping. Old school R&B is playing softly from a speaker. A couple of older men sit at the counter talking politics like they are personally responsible for saving the country.

Before we even make it three steps in, the woman behind the counter looks up and smiles widely when she sees Donovan.

"Well, look who done decided to show his face," she says, just like a woman who feels neglected would say.

He grins. "Morning, Mrs. Mary."

She wipes her hands on her apron and walks around the counter like she's known him his whole life. "You late today. I was about to give your seat away."

"Had to take care of some business," he says, flashing his eyes down at me.

Her eyes follow his. They land on me and soften instantly, the way Black women do when they clock another Black woman and decide, in half a second, that you are safe.

"Well, hey there, baby," she says. "Who is this pretty lady you brought with you, Donnie?"

Donovan gestures toward me. "This is Amina Ali. I owe her some very good breakfast, so I decided to bring her here."

She smiles, "Pretty name. Y'all go sit down now."

We slide into the booth near the window. The old vinyl seats squeak when I sit down, but I don't even care. Donovan slides deeper into the booth, stretching his arms along the back like it's his designated spot, which, clearly, it is. He obviously knows Mrs. Mary pretty well, so I'm sure there's more to the story.

"I've been coming here for years," he says casually. "My grandmother used to bring me when I was little. Back when this place had them ugly orange booths, and the cook smoked cigarettes in the kitchen like it was nothing."

I laugh. "That explains why everybody here knows you by name."

Mrs. Mary reappears with a notepad, already nodding like the order is halfway written in her head.

"Alright, Donnie," she says. "Same thing?"

"You already know," he says. "Bacon, egg, and cheese. Buttered white bread with jelly, and a side of grits."

She nods, like her body remembered without her brain needing confirmation, then turns to me. "And you, baby?"

"I'll do the waffles, eggs, and turkey sausage," I say.

She smiles. "I can do that."

When she walks off, I look at Donovan. "That order was very specific."

He shrugs. "It's my go-to for sure," he says. "Some things don't need changing."

I nod in agreement. That makes sense to me.

We sit there talking about nothing and everything at the same time. From Amberline Heights to the job, to how much the city has changed over the years. Gentrification sure is an interesting thing. Talking to Donovan is easy. Almost too easy. Like the universe gave me a soft moment on purpose, just to see what I would do with it.

Then I look up, and my stomach drops.

Akil.

My baby brother...

He's standing near the counter, hoodie pulled down low, hands shoved in his pockets. He looks thinner than the last time I saw him. Not skinny but worn down. His eyes are bloodshot red. Not tired red. Not allergy red. High as hell red. I keep telling him to stop smoking so much damn weed.

My face looks distraught, and Donovan notices the shift in me immediately.

"What are you looking at?" he asks.

I don't answer right away. I'm too busy looking at Akil. I watch him walk up to the register, laugh at something the cashier says, like nothing in the world is wrong. And knowing him, he'll tell you that nothing is wrong. The only thing Akil cares about is money and women.

"That's my baby brother," I say finally. "Akil."

Donovan follows my gaze. "Okay..."

"I haven't seen him in like six or seven months," I say, my voice quieter now. "He typically just disappears for a while."

Before Donovan can respond, Akil looks up and spots me.

His face lights up instantly.

"Amina," he says, already moving toward us.

I stand up as he reaches for me and wraps me in a familiar hug.

"What's up, big sis," he says, pulling me into his shoulder.

I squeeze him tighter than usual because I missed him, then pull back and look him up and down.

"Akil," I say. "What's up, bro? Where have you been? You haven't called anyone. Not me. Not Grandma."

He shrugs, eyes shifting away. "Man, I been around."

Around where? Doing what? With who? All the questions crowd my throat, but before I can ask them, the cashier calls his name.

"Akil, your order is ready."

He flinches.

"That's me," he says quickly, already stepping away. He looks back at me. "I gotta go, sis."

"Akil, wait," I say. "Why are you not coming around? You know Grandma is worried about you."

"I said I gotta go," he cut in, not angry or anything, just closed off. "I'll hit you later."

He gives me a quick nod, then turns and grabs his food, disappearing out the door before I can say anything else.

I sit back down slowly. My appetite is suddenly gone. Donovan watches without saying anything at first, giving me space.

Finally, he asks gently, "Why doesn't he come around?

I sigh, staring out the window. "I wish I knew. Akil has been lost for a while now. Ever since my mom and my dad died, he's been lost."

Donovan nods slowly. "Well, that kind of pain doesn't disappear on its own," he says. Then he pauses, choosing his words carefully. "Especially for men. A lot of us don't know how to even recognize that we're hurting, let alone say it out loud. We're taught to keep it moving. We're taught to keep it together and act like there's nothing wrong."

I guess I've never really thought about it like that.

"No one ever really asks men how they're doing," he continues. "And when they do get asked, most men don't feel safe enough to answer honestly. So, it comes out sideways. It often is expressed as anger or distance."

I look down at my plate, "That sounds exactly like Akil."

Donovan's voice softens. "It doesn't mean he doesn't care. Sometimes it just means he doesn't know how to come back yet."

I don't respond. I just look out the window and watch the cars pass. Donovan just put words to something I've been struggling to explain for years.

Finally, our food comes out. Mrs. Mary sets our plates down, and that's what finally pulls me back into the moment. The food looks too good to ignore. Golden waffles stacked just right, butter already melting into the pockets. The eggs are soft and perfect, and the grits look like somebody's auntie was back there stirring with love. I pull my phone out without even thinking and snap a picture. A day party brunch plate could never compete with this. No DJ, no overpriced mimosas, just real, homemade comfort sitting right in front of me.

Donovan looks at me, amused. "You good?"

"Yeah," I say.

The heaviness from the interaction with Akil eases with each bite I take. The taste of butter and hot syrup brings me all the way back into the incredible time I'm having with the gorgeous man who sits in front of me. Donovan takes a bite and nods like the food just validated his entire life.

"Still undefeated," he says.

I smile. "You were definitely right. This place is legit."

"I told you so," he says. You have got to trust a brotha sometimes."

"Sometimes, huh?"

After a few bites, I sit up a little straighter, letting my brain shift gears. "So," I say, "my concept for SPARK is actually going well."

He looks up, immediately attentive. "Yeah?"

"I finally feel confident about it," I say. "However, I caught Lucas snooping through my notes the other day. He was literally sitting at my desk as if he belonged there."

Donovan's jaw tightens, just enough to notice that he's clearly feeling some type of way.

"Well," he says calmly, "that tells me everything I need to know."

I lock eyes with him. "Do tell."

"That he's intimidated by you,' he says without hesitation.

I shake my head and let out a breath, "It's frustrating."

"I know," he says, "but don't let that get you off your game. Keep doing what you're doing. People like him get loud when they feel themselves getting left behind." He pauses, then continues. "Just stay aware. I don't like Lucas either, I deal with him."

"I believe in you," he adds. "For real."

"Thank you," I say quietly.

We finish eating, the conversation drifting back into lighter territory without effort. Jokes that spiral into laughter, stories that start at one place and end somewhere else. Somewhere in there, I find out that

Donovan, built like he could wrestle a small bear, is absolutely terrified of monkeys. I laugh so hard I have to put my fork down, and he just shakes his head, pretending he did not give me premium information I will absolutely use against him later.

When we step outside, the air is warmer now, the sun sitting higher in the sky. We walk toward his truck, side by side, bodies close. It feels like the day is giving us grace on purpose.

"I'll take you home," he says.

The ride back is quiet in a good way. Kendrick still vibrates through the speakers. The city looks rather peaceful this morning, like it exhaled overnight. When we pull up in front of Grandma Jamila's, he puts the Tahoe in park but doesn't rush the moment.

"You good?" he asks.

"Yeah," I say. "I am."

I thank him for the amazing morning, grab my bag, and step out of the car. The door shuts behind me with a soft click.

Then, I hear the window roll down.

"Amina."

I stop and turn around.

He leans across the passenger seat, one arm resting casually like this isn't a moment he's been thinking about too. His voice drops just enough to make it feel private.

"Hey," he says. "We should do this again."

I smile, just enough to let him know I feel it too.

"I think we should," I say.

I turn around and walk toward the front door of the house, the smile still sitting on my face.

I don't look back this time.

I don't have to, because I can already feel him looking at me.

8

Humble Mondays

Most people who work an office job hate Mondays. It's the start of a new week, and potentially new troubles. Monday mornings have a way of humbling you. They are supposed to be practical and purposeful, primed for survival and coffee, not seduction.

Today though...

Today, it's Monday, and I'm bringing sexy with me. Not raunchy, not pressed for attention, just subtle notes of seduction sprinkled here and there, throughout the day. I'm talking about that quiet, grown woman type of sexy. The type of sexy that doesn't beg for recognition, but pulls it in quietly, like gravity.

The type that makes people feel your energy before they ever actually see you. Sure, I'd be lying if I said Donovan doesn't have anything to do with it. Of course he does. I'm still riding the high from our amazing, quote-unquote, jogging date.

I take my time getting dressed. I don't rush; I let the moment stretch a little. Stalling, as Grandma Jamila would call it. I put on slacks that hug my hips without clinging too tightly. A silk blouse that hugs my figure so eloquently. Heels that say I came prepared for whatever the day tries to throw at me.

My hair is laid, and my makeup is soft and luminous. My lips are glossy enough to catch the light when I speak, but soft enough to be palatable if I were to suddenly be kissed by a prince.

Then I reach for my perfume. I knew I was buying it the second it hit my skin in that little shop at the mall. One inhale, and my spirit said, yeah... this one is coming home with me. I call it the *Man Trapper*, because it never misses the plot to make men look my way. Every time I wear it, men start acting like they're in heat and forget how to behave.

It's warm, slightly sweet, and a little animalic, bringing out my natural pheromones. It sits close to the skin like a secret, and blooms only when someone gets near enough to deserve it, slowly inviting curiosity.

I spray it behind my ears, along my wrists, and just once across my chest. Just enough to do the job.

Today, I don't want to disappear into Monday like I usually do. Nah. Today I want to own that shit. I want Monday to be my bottom bitch, doing whatever I say, moving when I move, completely falling in line. I want all eyes to be on me. I want the day to feel me when I walk in and remember I was here.

When I walk into OHE & Associates, the whole place gets robbed in broad daylight. My plan is working like a damn heist, clean execution, no remorse. I'm not asking for attention, I'm taking it, and everyone in here feels it whether they like it or not. Heads snap, and everyone is looking at me a little longer than usual. I guess taking that extra time to be intentionally sexy works in my favor. Today, I didn't come in meek; I came in tailored, intentional, fine as hell, and fully aware of it.

"Good morning, Amina... Ms. Ali," Stacy says, her smile carrying something a little extra with it today.

"Good morning," I reply, already aware and confident.

I'm almost at my cubicle when I feel it.

The awareness in the room. *Damn,* the spotlight really is on me.

Yeah, this is exactly the shit I was looking for.

Donovan is standing by the coffee station, mug in hand, mid-conversation with a colleague. His eyes find mine. His gaze drifts towards my outfit, controlled but curious, then returns to my face. He doesn't smile right away, but then he does. It's not big, but it says he noticed everything and plans to keep it to himself. He winks and me and slightly bites his bottom lip.

I make it to my desk and sit down, crossing my legs, like I don't know what I'm doing.

Buzz.

My phone lights up.

Okay... did I ever tell you how fine you are?

I just sit there and bite my lip. He's part of the reason why I did this.

Good morning to you too, Mr. Davis.

That perfume? I smell it all the way down the hall. I'm struggling to focus.

Maybe that was the intention.

Interesting.

Focus, Amina.

So, I think we need to go over SPARK today. From what I'm hearing, we're going to be asked to present our concepts soon.

Alright, we can do that.

We book one of the smaller conference rooms for later that afternoon. Donovan gets there first. When I walk in, he's standing by the window, sleeves rolled up just enough to make any woman notice. His laptop is already open, papers neat, everything about him saying prepared, but the way his shoulders square when he notices me gives him away. His posture is relaxed but alert, like a man trying extremely hard to keep his thoughts where they belong. At this point, I think we're both trying to hard to keep things professional.

"Hey", he says.

"Hey," I respond, closing the door behind me.

For a second, neither of us moves. Not awkward, just aware. The air feels heavier than it should for a meeting about a work presentation, but here we are.

"Ready?" he asks, clearing his throat slightly.

"Yeah," I say, stepping closer to the table.

I connect my laptop to the screen and pull up my slide deck. The title appears on the screen.

A SPARK Through Time.

Donovan's eyes move from the screen to me. "I like that."

"It felt right," I say. "SPARK isn't just an event. It's a marker. I wanted the presentation to feel like you're watching a journey."

I move through the first section. I have slides on OHE & Associates' early partnerships, notable projects, and archival photos layered with clean, modern graphics.

"This section establishes credibility," I explain. "Where SPARK started, what it was meant to do, and why it mattered then."

Donovan steps closer to the screen, hands in his pockets. He's standing close enough now that I'm aware of his presence without looking directly at him. Hmm, he smells good.

"And this?" he asks, pointing to a section I haven't explained yet.

I click forward.

"This is where we show evolution," I say. "Not just growth for growth's sake, but intentional expansion. The kind of expansion that signals true leadership and real vision."

He nods slowly. "Nice... you're telling a story with data."

"Exactly," I say. "People remember stories. The data just backs those stories up."

I move to the final section.

"This part," I say, my voice a little softer, "is about what SPARK becomes next. I want to have interactive elements and QR codes tied to specific future projects. I also think it would be dope to have testimonials from past clients to connect the past to what we're building today."

Donovan turns toward me fully now.

"You're not just highlighting a past win," he says. "You're positioning OHE as unstoppable."

I meet his eyes and don't rush to look away.

"That was the goal."

The pause that follows isn't awkward. It isn't uncomfortable either. It's more like a pregnant pause, as the room fills with tension.

"You know," he says, lowering his voice just slightly, "this is senior-level thinking."

I feel an immense amount of contentment. "That actually means a lot coming from you, Donovan," I say. "You don't strike me as the type to gas people up just to be nice."

"I'm not, and mean what I said," he says. "For what it's worth... Lucas snooping through your notes makes complete sense now."

I smile faintly. "You think so?"

"I know so," he says. "People don't hover around ideas and people they're not scared of."

He leans closer to the table, bracing himself with one hand. I shift my position without thinking, suddenly aware of how close we are. The screen keeps running, the only thing breaking the silence between us. I want to lean in more, but I have to silently remind myself that we're at work.

"You good with the pacing here?" he asks, gesturing to the slide, his arm brushing mine just barely.

"Yeah," I say, my breath steady. "I want it to feel confident and unrushed."

"Like you look," he says before he can stop himself.

Our eyes lock.

For a second, it feels like we're standing on the edge of a cliff. Not falling, but that feeling right before you jump. I feel an overwhelming amount of adrenaline shoot through my entire body.

He straightens, resetting the distance. "You're ready, Amina."

I nod. "Thank you."

OHE has been a little rough. My first true corporate experience hasn't been easy, but finally, I don't feel like I'm constantly fixing myself or proving anything.

I feel like I've arrived, and Donovan's approval is only confirmation.

When we pack up and walk out of the conference room, Donovan keeps his voice low, professional, but it's sensual.

"You're going to crush your SPARK presentation," he says.

I smile, small but certain. "Oh, I plan to."

We part ways at the split in the hall, both of us headed back to our cubicles as if nothing happened. I reach my desk, my mind already running through tweaks and timing. As I set my bag down, voices carry over from the break area a few feet away. I've always been a little nosy, so I move a little closer without being seen.

It's Lucas and Anna.

I don't mean to listen so intently, but I hear my name come up. I already know where this is going. If there's one thing I can't stand, it's people who can't say shit to your face but love to get brave when you're not in the room.

"She seems... confident," Anna says, her tone measured in that careful way people use when they think they're being fair.

Lucas lets out a small laugh under his breath. "Confident is one word."

There's a pause.

"I just wonder," Anna adds, lowering her voice, "if her presentation might be... too cultured."

She loves that fucking word. Too cultured. Yeah right.

Lucas sighs in agreement. "Yeah. I mean, SPARK is a corporate event. We have to be mindful of our audience."

My face tightens, but my hands stay on my keyboard.

I exhale slowly through my nose. Back in the day, this would constitute the need for all of us to square up, however, I know that things are different now. Years of practice have taught me that reacting in real time rarely does me any favors. I know better than to spaz out right here, especially not over people who want a reaction more than they want results. So, I keep my eyes on my screen, scrolling through emails that I'm honestly not really reading at this point.

Then, right on cue, I receive an email from Ben. I click it open, because I have a feeling this is about our presentations.

From: Ben Kowalski

Subject: SPARK Presentation Schedule

Hi Team,

I wanted to confirm that Anna, Lucas, and Amina will each be presenting their SPARK concepts this Friday at 10:00 a.m. Please clear your schedules for two hours.

Anna, Lucas, and Amina, we are looking forward to seeing your work.

Best,

Ben

I lean back in my chair, hands resting on the armrests, mind already moving. It's the same feeling I get when I'm three steps ahead, and nobody else knows it yet. Like a queenpin planning her next move, calm because the board is already set.

Okay, Friday. So, this is what we're doing.

Donovan thinks I'm ready. And if I'm being honest with myself, I think I am too. Grandma Jamila didn't raise me to be a coward or scared. She raised me to always come prepared, to stand ten toes down, and to finish what I start.

They can call it too confident. They can call it too cultured. They can whisper about shit all they want. On Friday, I'm coming to win.

And I'm making my concept the one they choose.

9

The Pressure Cooker

By Wednesday, my whole body feels like a pressure cooker full of collard greens that somebody forgot about on the stove. The pot is just bubbling and hissing. One wrong move, and it'll be exploding all over the damn kitchen.

Pressure like this sits heavy in your shoulders, your jaw, and your lower back. I feel the weight of all my tears, all my grandmother's prayers, and everything that I could potentially lose or gain. This kind of pressure makes even blinking feel like too much effort. Friday is coming whether I'm ready or not, sitting heavy on my chest like an overdue bill, or like that time my long-lost auntie showed up at Grandma Jamila's house, and started critiquing everything before she even made it to the couch.

I've been at OHE & Associates for three months now. Long enough to know the pulse of the place. Long enough to recognize the inner office politics. Long enough to tell the difference between collaboration and competition. Long enough to feel confident enough to say this, even if only to myself.

I've earned my spot here. I'm just as capable as everyone else in this building, if not more. I also know the unspoken part. That because I'm Black, the margin of error is slimmer. The standard is higher. The effort has to be doubled, sometimes tripled, just to be seen as equal. Nobody hands you the benefit of the doubt like they do everyone else. Instead, you have to earn it, over and over again.

So, I get to the office early on purpose, as many days as I can. When it's early, the building is so quiet, it grants me the ability to let my thoughts be focused, instead of tripping over everybody else's noise. Just me and my thoughts is a perfect melody for success. It reminds me of track meets back in high school and college, waking up before the sun, lacing my shoes in the dark, already locked in. I knew back then that you didn't win races at the starting line; you won them in all the moments you prepared. I promised myself I'd carry that same discipline with me wherever I went, even if it was off the track. Excellence is the standard, no matter the arena.

Right now, the arena is SPARK.

I open my laptop and stare at the title slide.

A SPARK Through Time

I've looked at this slide deck a hundred times, but today it feels exposed. Like it's not just a presentation anymore, but a mirror. I'm not simply pitching an idea. I'm pitching something that could change the trajectory of my career. I worked my ass off making this slide deck. Every slide is clean. Every transition makes sense. Still, I find myself asking if good is good enough. I wonder if I'm being arrogant for believing my concept deserves to reign supreme over Lucas' and Anna's. Am I being overzealous for believing it could be chosen?

And... that's when it creeps in.

The doubt.

Black women know this feeling all too well. Imposter syndrome hits us differently. It's not just second-guessing your work; it's being hyper-aware of how few people in the room look like you. It's knowing that mistakes aren't just mistakes. It's an understanding that excellence is the baseline, not the exception. That you don't get the luxury of being average or experimental. Sometimes I wish I could just exist. Sometimes the pressure feels like too much. It's so hard not to question yourself when the world already does.

Am I doing too much? Is this too ambitious for someone with "Junior" in their title? Who do you think you are to reimagine something that's existed for twenty years?

I lean back in my chair and close my eyes because I've felt this before.

Brown.

Walking into classrooms where I was one of maybe two Black students, sometimes the only one. Surrounded by classmates who didn't look like me, and spoke so confidently about internships, legacy admissions, and opportunities that felt worlds away from where I came from. I didn't know anything about all of that.

And there I was, carrying all of it. The doubt, the fear, the weight, still showing up anyway, despite all of the emotions. Still showing up because that was the best option.

A chocolate, Black woman from the hood. Locs down my back, smelling like vanilla and cocoa butter. I didn't have a safety net. I didn't have a family blueprint for navigating elite spaces. I've never had mommy and daddy to lead the way and call in favors on my behalf. Just me, my work ethic, my poise, and my quiet refusal to fail.

Back then, I questioned whether I belonged every single day. Not because I wasn't capable, but because the environment kept reminding me that I was different. That I was an outlier. That I was unexpected. Something they hadn't planned for. Still, I did what needed to be done. I graduated with honors.

And now, here I am again. It's a different building, and the circumstances are different, but the feeling is the same.

Imposter syndrome doesn't always kick the door in like police on a drug bust. Sometimes it comes silent and precise, like a sniper posted up in the distance. One clean shot to your confidence, then suddenly, you're questioning things.

Suddenly, Brown feels distant. My master's degree feels theoretical. My accomplishments shrink in my mind like they belong to someone else.

I scroll through the deck faster now. The slides feel too bold and too confident. My cursor hovers over one section, and for a split second, I consider toning it down. Maybe I should make it safe and more palatable to the likings of others.

Then, my phone buzzes.

You're in early.

Hmm, I didn't see him come in yet.

Couldn't sleep. Friday is literally giving me insomnia.

I see. Want coffee?

Sure.

Five minutes later, he's standing at my cubicle with two cups. He hands one to me without hesitation. *Hmm, butter pecan, my favorite.*

"You, okay?" he asks quietly.

I nod out of habit, then stop myself.

"Honestly... I don't know," I say. "I keep second-guessing everything about this presentation."

He leans against the cubicle wall, and I can tell he's really trying to be supportive. "Talk to me."

"What if I'm doing too much?" I admit. "Lucas and Anna have been here for way longer than I have. They know how this place works, and what leadership would want. What if my idea doesn't land the way I think it will?"

He studies me and my facial expression for a moment. "Is that what you actually believe," he asks, "or is that what this environment is training you to believe?"

I don't respond right away.

"I've seen your work, and it's good," he continues. "That deck didn't come out of thin air. That shows just how brilliant your mind is."

"But it's..."

He cuts me off before I can finish my statement. "Self-doubt shows up when you're leveling up, especially for people like us. Not because you don't belong, but because you're expanding into spaces that weren't designed with you in mind. I think you're just getting started."

I look down at my coffee. My reflection wavers on the surface, distorted, like it's trying to decide who it wants to be today.

"I don't want to mess this up," I whisper, feeling like I could cry.

"You won't," he says. "And even if it doesn't go exactly how you picture it, that doesn't erase your brilliance. You already did the work. You already showed up. I know you can do this."

His words calm my mind just enough.

Later that morning, during a team check-in, Lucas dominates the conversation, seasoning every sentence with corporate buzzwords. When it's my turn, I speak clearly and confidently, but I don't do too much.

Afterward, Anna pulls me aside. "Your idea is... bold," she says carefully.

"That's intentional," I reply.

By the afternoon, the self-doubt hasn't disappeared yet, however, it's not driving anymore. It's riding quietly in the backseat. I tweak the deck to sharpen it, not soften it or change the intent of my presentation.

Before I leave for the day, my phone buzzes. It's Donovan again.

Don't tone it down. Friday is ready for you.

I respond to him with a smiley face emoji.

The train ride home is quieter than usual. Not because it's not full of people, but because my mind finally slows down enough to notice the city outside the window. By the time we reach my stop, I feel normal again. I get off and begin the walk home, and I spot a sign posted at one of the bus stops.

A sign advertising a new apartment complex, not too far from Grandma Jamila's. I surely didn't see this when I went to look at places before.

NOW LEASING
NEW CONSTRUCTION
TWO MONTHS FREE

I've let a couple more checks stack to make me feel a little more prepared to move and get an apartment. That alone makes me curious. Curious enough to get on a bus and go see what this place is all about.

When I walk into the leasing office, the first thing I notice is how bright it is. It's clean, but not sterile, and it smells like fresh paint. The leasing agent greets me with a smile so familiar, I almost want to call her cousin. She tells me the building just opened two weeks ago. It sure would be nice to move into a unit that no one else has lived in.

She gives me a tour of one of the available units. The floors are luxury vinyl, and the sunlight pours in and illuminates the entire unit with warm natural light. The kitchen is nice, and I could imagine myself cooking breakfast every weekend in here. The leasing agent mentions the special again, two months free, with a move-in date about four weeks out.

I think about the last three months at OHE & Associates. The confidence I've built brick by brick. The late nights, the early mornings, and the steady coin I've managed to put aside. I'm actually proud of myself for these small feats. I should be able to reward myself, shouldn't I? At some point, decisions stop being a debate, and they become choices.

Fuck it.

I sign the lease.

When I step back outside the complex, I take a deep breath and let it out slowly. Forward motion feels good when you choose it instead of waiting for permission.

When I finally get home, I tell Grandma Jamila the news.

"I got an apartment," I say.

There's a pause, then a sigh. "I'm proud of you, Mina," she says. "I'm just gonna miss having you around."

"Grandma, I'll be right up the street... I'll still come by and spend the night sometimes," I promise.

That night, I sit on my bed with my laptop open, SPARK glowing back at me like it knows what's coming. I shake my head and laugh under my breath at myself.

Damn Amina...

New job. New apartment. I wonder what's next. One milestone at a time. One win stacked on top of another. I'm proud of myself, but I can't get too comfortable. At least not yet.

First, I must tackle Friday.

And when Friday gets here, I'm not showing up to participate. I'm showing up to take what's mine.

10

The Moment of Truth

Friday is here.

It pulls up on me like a debt I can't dodge, blowing me up like a bill collector.

I lay in the bed, and my eyes finally open, but my body is already awake, already bracing. My heart is thumping like it knows something important is happening. Not from fear exactly, but from knowing today is about to pull something out of me. This isn't just nerves. This is anticipation mixed with consequence. The type of nerves that make you lie still for a second longer, just long enough to gather yourself before the world starts demanding answers.

So... I oblige.

I stay in my bed for a moment longer, staring at the ceiling, letting all the feelings inside me do their thing. Today isn't just about a presentation; it's about proving myself. Not only do I need to prove myself to OHE & Associates, but I also need to prove myself to me.

Today is the day I find out if it was all worth it. If all the late nights, the bullshit, and quiet resilience finally add up to something tangible. It's been three months since I started at OHE & Associates. Three months of learning how to move, how to speak, and how to exist in a space that didn't exactly make room for me but... couldn't deny me either. Today feels like a mirror, so whatever looks back at me, I have to be ready to face it.

Finally, I sit up.

"Alright," I whisper to myself. "Let's do this shit."

I take my time getting ready because today I want to look like a motherfucking boss. Not the boss you second-guess. Not the boss you talk over in meetings. I want to look like the kind of boss that walks in and changes the temperature of the room like a damn meteorologist, and makes people adjust their posture without knowing why. Today, I want it to be clear that I did not come to play, to participate, or to be grateful for a seat at the motherfucking table. I came to own the space, collect what's mine, and leave a mark.

I slide into a fitted black blazer that feels like an executive decision all by itself, sharp shoulders framing me like I'm about to close a deal that increases somebody's balance sheet. The fabric hugs with authority, tailored like it knows I mean business. My heels announce me before my voice does, a steady percussion that says I'm planted, I'm prepared, and I'm not backing down to anyone. I pull my hair into a sleek ponytail so that my face stays forward and nothing distracts the audience from what I came to deliver. My makeup is soft, but lethal, polished enough for the boardroom, and precise enough to remind me who I am when I catch my reflection. This is not about being pretty or palatable. This is about armor you can't see, strategy you can't steal, and a woman who knows exactly what she wants.

I add a touch of perfume. Not too much, but just enough so you smell me before you see me. I want it lingering in the air like a memory someone can't place right away.

I'm not trying to distract anyone, but I'm also not interested in going unnoticed. I'm trying to command the room. And if, somewhere in the middle of all that authority, Donovan happens to notice, then that would simply be a bonus. I'm not pretending otherwise.

I call a rideshare instead of taking the Metro because this outfit is not built for platform delays, urine-soaked floors, or seats that look like they've lived too many lives before me. I'm not squeezing past somebody arguing with an invisible enemy or holding my breath between stops while the train crawls through a tunnel it has no business stalling in today. I worked too hard for this moment to arrive wrinkled, rattled, or smelling like somebody else's bad night. I need my clothes to be on point, and my head to be clear when I walk through those doors.

By the time I step into OHE & Associates, the energy in the building is lit. It's chaotic, like a production set right before cameras start rolling. You can feel the energy before anyone says a word. People are moving fast, phones pressed to ears, and heels clicking all around the office. I straighten my shoulders and move through it like I belong here, because I do.

"Good morning, Amina," Stacy says from the front desk.

"Good morning," I reply, calm on the outside, but so nervous on the inside.

I head straight to my cubicle and pull up my slide deck one last time. I don't change anything. I told myself, no last-minute edits and no panicked tweaks. I've learned that confidence sometimes looks like leaving things exactly as they are.

I open my email, and there's a message from Ben. I open it immediately.

From: Ben Kowalski

Subject: SPARK Presentation Order and Timing

Thank you again for your work on your SPARK concepts. I wanted to confirm the presentation order and timing for today.

Lucas York will present first at 10:00 a.m. Anna Russo will present at 10:30 a.m. Amina Ali will present at 11:00 a.m.

Please plan to arrive at the big conference room ten minutes prior to your scheduled time. Presentations will be conducted individually.

Looking forward to seeing what you all have come up with.

Best,

Ben

My stomach is doing backflips.

I glance at the clock and feel my stomach twist and turn. There is still too much time left, which only gives my nerves more room to act up. Waiting has always been harder than doing, because waiting leaves space for doubt to start talking crazy to me.

At 9:50 a.m., Lucas heads toward the conference room. I watch him stroll past my desk with his chest out and his confidence on full display, as if he already knows the ending and likes how it turns out. He moves the way men do when the world has been saying yes to them for a long time. When he comes back out, the smile on his face looks almost cinematic, like the villain at the end of a movie who knows something the rest of us do not. He's too calm and too satisfied, almost as if he just walked away from a crime scene, knowing that he did the crime, and also knowing that no one noticed.

Anna goes next. She glides, not rushes, toward the conference room, composed and unbothered. She moves like someone who has always had a seat at the table, and the rules were explained to her early and reinforced often. There's an ease in her posture that comes from familiarity, from growing up believing the system will catch you when you fall instead of letting you hit the ground. She disappears into the conference room without looking back.

Then there's me...

I sit at my desk with my laptop closed and my hands folded like I'm trying to keep myself together by force. I am literally dying inside. My chest is tight, and I feel like I can't breathe. I wonder if this is what people with asthma feel like. I don't open my slide deck again. I already know it front to back, and I learned a long time ago that staring at your work right before something big only makes doubt feel louder than preparation.

Instead, my mind drifts somewhere else.

Brown.

I'm standing at the front of a lecture hall during my sophomore year, hands shaking so badly I had to grip the podium just to stay upright. There was a room full of strangers staring back at me. Professors in the front row. My voice was cracking on the first sentence.

I remember thinking, they're about to see right through me. They're not going to like my presentation. They're going to know I don't belong here.

And then something snapped inside of me.

I remembered my material. Then, I remembered how much time I spent researching my material. I remembered how confident I was in the research. Then I remembered why I was there. Long story short,

I finished that presentation that day and passed with flying colors. I walked back to my seat lightheaded but proud of myself. The next day, the professor stopped me after class and told me that my presentation was excellent. I didn't expect the praise, but it made me feel good.

I remind myself of that now. I'm the same woman, with the same mind, it's just a different room.

At 10:50 a.m., I stand up from my desk. I smooth my blazer, grab my laptop, and head toward the conference room. My heels echo softly down the hall. I don't rush, but I don't stall either. I'm walking into something I already decided belongs to me, so my body language should exude that.

When I reach the door, Ben opens it with a smile.

"Ready?" he asks.

I nod. "Yes."

Inside, the room is quiet. It almost reminds me of the silence in a church service, right before the preacher gives the sermon. It's just Ben, Tony, a long table sitting there like a judge, and a blank screen staring back at me, daring me to fill it with something memorable.

I reach for the HDMI cord and connect my laptop to the screen. My heart is beating fast, like a bass line in my chest, loud enough to throw me off if I let it. I pull my breath back in, reminding myself that I've stood in rooms like this before.

"Good morning," I begin. "Thank you for taking the time today to hear my concept."

I click the first slide.

A SPARK Through Time

I don't rush or overperform. I take my time and explain my thinking the way it deserves to be explained. I walk them through the foundation of SPARK, not selling a gimmick but laying down a philosophy. I root it in intention and impact, in why it matters and why it fits here. My words are clean and controlled, not flashy, because flash fades and clarity sticks.

When I get to the data, I slow it down even more. I really talk them through it in the most professional way. I explain why every metric exists and what it's accountable for. I talk about how growth without direction is just noise, and how SPARK has to grow up and evolve the same way OHE & Associates itself has grown.

Out of the corner of my eye, I notice Tony nodding. When I move to the experiential elements, I see Ben lean forward in his chair. That tells me everything I need to know. Leaning forward is typically a good indicator of interest.

I walk them through my ideas, making sure to highlight the timelines, the QR station, the flow of the experience, and how people should feel through it. I tell them this isn't about nostalgia for nostalgia's sake. This is about continuity, about honoring where OHE & Associates has been, while making it clear where it is going next.

When I finish presenting my slide deck, the questions come. They're direct, thoughtful, and a little challenging. I answer every question without rambling or shrinking, holding my ground like I built it myself. By the time we wrap up, my nerves have finally settled, and I feel pretty cool.

"Thank you, Amina," Ben says. "That was very thorough."

Tony nods.

I calmly gather my things and walk out of the conference room with my posture intact, even though my heart is beating like I just ran a mile I didn't train for. The moment the door closes behind me, the adrenaline starts to dissipate, and by the time I sit back down at my desk, my mind is already running tape like a late-night highlight reel. I replay every question, every pause, every answer, and I start wondering if I should have pushed one idea harder or said anything a little better.

My phone buzzes.

You were incredible.

I pause and stare at my phone.

Incredible how?

A few seconds pass.

Poised, clear, and you didn't rush. You owned that shit.

Wait… how did you know all of that?

There's a longer pause this time.

Okay, don't be mad…

Donovan…

I was listening.

Listening where?

At the door. I couldn't help myself. I told myself I was just walking by, and then you started talking, so I stayed to listen.

I shake my head, smiling.

OMG, that is so embarrassing. You're ridiculous lol.

I'm serious, Amina. You sounded like somebody who knew exactly why she was standing in that room. Not nervous. Not trying to impress, just sure of yourself.

Thank you. I really needed to hear that.

Anytime. I meant what I said. You didn't have to do this alone.

I set my phone face down on my desk, letting the moment marinate. Knowing Donovan is in my corner does something to me that feels better than adrenaline and warmer than praise. A man like him in my corner is always a good thing.

Whatever this thing is between us, it's still wrapped tight in professionalism, pressed and tailored like a suit you only wear when the stakes are real. But it exists, and I feel better knowing that he saw me clearly today and approves of my presentation.

The rest of the afternoon drags. I answer some emails and read over some campaigns, but my mind keeps circling back to that room. That moment. That voice that didn't shake. That was all me.

When I get home, Grandma Jamila asks how it went.

"I think I did okay," I say.

"That's all you can do, baby. The rest is waiting," she says.

She sings, as if she's singing an old Negro spiritual. Her voice carries the weight of lived-in wisdom, of prayers said over kitchen tables, and hard years survived through numerous trials and tribulations. She reassures me that I showed up the way I was supposed to, that I handled my responsibility with grace, and the rest is not mine to wrestle with. She reminds me that timing is its own kind of teacher, and you cannot rush what is meant to be.

So, I wait...

For what it's worth, Friday will decide what it decides.

11

Truth on Trial

Monday meets me at the door like it knows what I survived. Not gentle, not apologetic, just standing there daring me to remember that I made it through Friday in one piece. My shoulders feel lighter, not because anything has been decided, but because the waiting room in my chest has finally emptied out. The presentation already happened. The words already left my mouth. The room already heard me. Whatever comes next cannot undo that.

I walk into work knowing that I didn't bend or fold. I didn't stutter or shrink myself into something more digestible. I didn't let what Lucas or Anna said deter me. No more rehearsing statements in my head like a public defender on a caffeine binge. No more pacing in my bedroom at night, whispering slide notes to the walls as if they might testify for me. Friday ran its course, and I walked out standing.

The weekend helped too. Grandma Jamila and I went grocery shopping Saturday morning, and it was lovely. We moved through each of the aisles like it was a church. She stopped every few feet to compare prices, squinting at labels like the store was trying to run game on her. I told her not to worry about it and loaded the cart because I could finally contribute, and that alone felt like a win. We got a chance to talk and catch up. I told her I ran into Akil again a while back. She didn't gasp or lecture me about it, she just sighed and said she's praying for him. Praying he finds his way back to himself and to us.

On Sunday, she made Maryland crab cakes, the real ones, where you can actually taste the crab, and not just the filler. The house smelled like comfort and memory, like kitchens where hard conversations still ended in food. Black folks sure love to eat. She also made that homemade dressing she refuses to write down, as if the recipe might lose power if it left her hands. We ate, we laughed, and the woes of the world stayed outside.

So yeah, Monday starts off decent. Hard not to, honestly. When your weekend was full of crabs being steamed and cracked open, fingers smelling like Old Bay, surrounded by good company, it's damn near impossible to come into work mad at the world. Hell, I even brought a crab cake with me for lunch, with two slices of white bread to make a nice little sandwich.

I walk into OHE & Associates, greet Stacy at the front desk, and head to my cubicle like it's any other morning. I get myself situated, open my laptop, and start answering emails. A little small talk here, a little research there. At this point, I am convinced that everything is fine and going just as it should.

Then I refresh my inbox.

From: Ben Kowalski

Subject: Quick Chat

Amina,

I need to speak with you this morning. Please come to my office in fifteen minutes.

Best,

Ben

For some reason, I have this sinking feeling in my stomach. Not because I've done anything wrong. Actually, I know for a fact that I haven't done anything wrong. Still, it's just something about being summoned without context that immediately puts you on edge. Fifteen minutes is just enough time to panic, but not enough time to prepare for whatever the conversation may be about. It's a countdown designed to let your imagination run wild.

I stare at my laptop screen.

Quick chat.

That phrase is a wildcard. It could mean anything. It could mean praise. It could mean clarification. It could mean that maybe I am in some type of trouble. For some reason, my gut doesn't like the way it's sitting.

I try to work, I really do. I answer a couple of emails, skim a document, and pretend to focus. Unfortunately, my mind keeps sprinting ahead of me, writing scenes in my head I never auditioned for. By the time I check the clock again, the fifteen minutes are gone.

I stand up, fix my blazer, and head toward Ben's office. I'm nervous, but I refuse to let my nerves lead. I haven't done shit wrong, and I will not enter the room acting like I did.

"Amina," Ben says when I walk in, his tone flatter than usual. "Have a seat, please."

I sit across from him, with my hands folded neatly in my lap.

"So," he begins, leaning back slightly, "your SPARK presentation was good."

That seems good, but I can't tell if that was a compliment or something else.

"However," he continues, "there were some strong similarities between your presentation and Lucas' presentation."

I give him this confused look. "Similarities, how?"

"Well," he says, glancing at his notes, "you titled yours *A SPARK Through Time*. Lucas titled his *SPARKLE Through Time*. Also, some of the concepts you presented were also included in his."

My chest tightens, and I shake my head as a wave of anger comes over me.

"I'm not sure how that would've happened," he adds, "unless you copied his work."

For a second, I just stare at him. I'm a mixture of confused and calculating my next move. Then my voice comes back, sharp and steady, the way it does when I refuse to be misunderstood.

"Copied him?" I repeat. "I would never."

Ben watches me closely, as if he's trying to decide which version of the story he believes.

"Actually," I continue, sitting up straighter, "did I mention that I caught Lucas at my desk snooping through my SPARK notes way before the presentation?"

That gets his attention. His eyebrows lift, just enough to show surprise, just enough to tell me this is new information. I don't mean to be a snitch, but when it comes to this, I will gladly tell it all.

"So, if anyone copied anything," I say calmly, "it wasn't me."

The room goes quiet. Ben leans back in his chair, steepling his fingers, studying me now instead of his notes.

"Interesting," he says.

No one speaks for a moment. The silent stretches and things get a little awkward.

Finally, Ben speaks. "We'll conduct an investigation," he says. "For now, you can return to your work."

That's it. No reassurance. No resolution. Just... dismissal.

I walk back to my cubicle on autopilot, staring straight ahead like I might combust if I look too closely at anyone. By the time I sit down, my hands are shaking, not from nerves, but from rage. I am so heated, my anger feels like if I take one wrong breath, I may spark a fire right in the middle of this office. This isn't just irritation or frustration; this is the kind of fury that demands restraint because it could be destructive if I let it loose.

This man really stole my fucking work. No wonder he walked out of his presentation looking so jolly. He had the audacity to take my idea, slap a new name on it, and present it like it was his, and now I'm the one sitting here under a microscope. I'm being questioned and treated like I might be the problem. Like I'm some sort of workplace criminal instead of the person who built the damn thing.

I don't even know where to take this or whom I can report this to. Human Resources feels too big and too clinical. Anna doesn't feel like a safe person to vent to. Ben seems like he's already decided that I'm the problem, so it's no point in trying to talk to him again.

So, I do the only thing that makes sense. I text Donovan.

Donovan…

A few seconds later.

Yes ma'am.

I just met with Ben. He thinks I copied my SPARK presentation from Lucas.

What!!!

Yesss.

That's wild. Especially since you caught him at your desk.

Exactly. I really don't want to get fired. I just signed an apartment lease.

Okay, okay. First of all, congratulations on the apartment. Second, slow down. I'm going to talk Ben and see what's up.

No, I don't want you getting involved. I don't want it to look messy.

Trust me. I'm not telling him you told me anything. I'm just going to see where his head is at. I'll make it seem like I want to know where everything is at with SPARK. Standby.

I lean back in my chair and stare at the ceiling, trying to keep myself from freaking out. The rest of the day drags on. I answer emails. I sit in on a couple of virtual meetings. I pretend to care about tasks that suddenly feel pointless if my job might be in jeopardy. My stomach stays in knots the entire time.

Three hours pass, then my phone buzzes.

Alright, Ben is definitely upset, but he did say he's going to conduct a thorough investigation. He'll probably ask me what I know. For now, just chill and let it play out.

I exhale for the first time all day.

Thank you, Donovan.

I sit there for a moment longer, trying to calm my nerves. I don't know how this ends. I don't know who they'll believe. All I know is that waiting feels worse than the accusation itself.

By the time I get home, I am huffing and puffing all the way inside the door, like I'm carrying the whole damn day on my back. My head is rocking so hard, my temples throb. It's not just a simple headache; it's pressure, stress, and disrespect balled up right behind my forehead. I don't have an appetite, I don't have the energy to fake a conversation, and I don't even have the energy to properly take my jacket off. I kick off my shoes by the door and drop my bag onto the first chair I see, loud enough for Grandma Jamila to hear it from the kitchen.

She's in the kitchen, standing over the stove, singing softly to herself like the world hasn't just tried to play in my face.

"You sound like somebody stole something from you," she says without turning around.

I let out one sharp laugh, all sarcasm and no humor. "Funny you say that, Grandma."

She finally turns around. "What happened?"

I sit at the table and tell her everything. The email, the conversation with Ben, the accusation. I tell her how Lucas stole my work and then stood there and played dumb, like coincidence could cover intention. By the time I finish explaining everything to her, my voice is cracked and thin. I continue anyway.

Grandma Jamila listens, I mean really opens her ears for me. She doesn't interrupt or try to rush to fix it. She just nods slowly, eyes locked on me, filing every word away for her response. When I finally run out of breath, she lets out a long sigh and pulls her chair across from mine.

"Baby," she says, "let me tell you something, honey."

I look at her.

"When I first started working as a secretary at that real estate company downtown, I was the only Black woman in the whole office. It wasn't even common for women to be working like that back then, especially not married women. Folks expected us to be at home, keep quiet, and depend on somebody else to carry us."

She pauses, fingers tracing the edge of the table, like she's grounding herself in the memory.

"But your grandfather was killed," she says softly. Just like that. One day he was here, next day I had three kids and no other options."

Tears spill out of my eyes before I can stop them.

"So, I went to work," she continues. "I had to. Phones ringing nonstop, papers stacked everywhere, white men in suits walking past me like I was invisible unless they needed something typed."

She shakes her head.

"There was this one woman," she says. "She sat two desks over from me. Every time I helped an agent clean up a deal or catch a mistake, she would repeat it in meetings like it was her idea, and they praised her for it. They said she was sharp."

My jaw clenches because I know the feeling.

"I learned real quick she wasn't smarter than me," Grandma Jamila says. "She was just comfortable stealing my praise and confident nobody would question it. Especially not me."

"So, what did you do?" I ask.

"I kept receipts," she says plainly. "Dates, notes, copies. I outworked her, not to prove myself to them, but to protect myself. Took time, but eventually folks started seeing the pattern. Truth always shows itself. Might take a minute, but it never stays hidden forever."

She reaches across the table and squeezes my hand.

"You did right by speaking up," she says. "Now you let it play out, child. Folks who steal do not rest easy. Folks who tell the truth usually sleep just fine."

She leans back slightly, studying my face.

"And listen to me real clear," she adds. "What they are doing to you is not new. It doesn't mean you messed up. It means you're standing in a room that was never built with you in mind, and they may not know what to do with your excellence right now."

Something about my grandmother's words always finds the ache and presses on it until it eases. Not because the problem disappears, but because she reminds me that I'm not carrying it alone. Her voice has a way of calming me, the same way it did when I was a child and scraped my knee or came home angry at the woes of a young girl growing up in Amberline Heights.

"You keep your head up," she says. "You tell the truth. You let them investigate, and you remember how I raised you. Remember the kind of woman I taught you to be. You do not bend yourself to make other folks comfortable. You do not be a coward when somebody tries to take what is yours. You stand tall, because you know who you are, always."

"Yes, Grandma," I respond.

After the conversation, I go upstairs and shut my bedroom door behind me. I don't bother turning on the lights. I head straight for the shower, because a hot shower has always been the closest thing to relief when I get headaches. The steam fills the bathroom fast and wraps around me the way I wish a man would when he knows I've had a long day and doesn't ask any questions.

I let the water fall heavy on my shoulders and feel the tension loosen with every drop, like it's being negotiated out of my body one muscle at a time. The water slides down my back, softening my neck, and all the places I've been holding tight out of habit. I breathe slower. For a few minutes, I let myself just exist under the nearly scolding water.

When I step out, I put on something soft and climb into bed, pulling the covers over me like armor, like a line drawn in chalk that says this is as far as today gets to go. Lucas is not invited here. Not his energy, not his nonsense, not even the thought of him. He does not get my night. He does not get my rest. I did nothing wrong, and I'm not dragging his mess into my peace like an unpaid bill.

Grandma Jamila's words float in my thoughts. I turn my face into the pillow. Tomorrow will come when it comes, and when it does, I will be ready.

12

In My Corner

Monday comes back around like it forgot we were tired of each other.

It drags itself into the day the way Grandma Jamila's old hoopty used to pull off in the morning, barely wanting to start. A full week has passed since the meeting with Ben, and I still have no answers. No updates. No follow-ups. Just deliberate, bureaucratic silence that lets you know someone is out there deciding your fate. I don't like the way it feels. Not knowing the fate or the outcome has been taxing on my mental health.

I show up to work anyway, despite how I'm feeling. I follow my same routine. I get on the same train. I walk into the same building. I do the same badge swipe that says I belong here, even when it feels like I'm on trial. My body moves on instinct, but my spirit feels encumbered, like I'm hauling an invisible weight nobody offered to help me carry. I smile when protocol demands it. I nod when spoken to. I do my job from repetition, instead of conviction. I catch myself wondering who has already made up their mind about me. I wonder if my name sounds different now when people say it. If it has traveled into rooms that I will never be invited to. I would put money on the fact that somebody has been talking shit about me.

I sit at my desk and scroll through emails until they blur together. Someone wants an update. Someone else needs clarification. Another person needs a guest list revised. All of it feels pointless when I don't even know if I'm going to have a damn job.

Then my screen pings.

My chest tightens. This could be it. This could be the truth finally stepping into the light, or this could be my reckoning.

From: Ben Kowalski

Subject: Quick Update

Amina,

I need to see you in my office for an update on the results of the investigation. You can come as soon as you see this.

Best,

Ben.

Oh shit.

My stomach drops so fast it feels like it skipped my ribs entirely and landed just at my ankles. There's no point in stalling. If I'm going to be terminated, he can tell me quickly so I can get on with my day. Plus, waiting only gives fear more time to run its mouth. I stand, adjust my blazer as usual, and head to Ben's office like I'm headed to hear my verdict in court.

"Amina," he says when I walk in. His tone is neutral. Unreadable, if I must say. "Please, have a seat."

I sit.

"Do you enjoy working here? He asks.

The question feels rather loaded, and I'm trying to understand the rationale. I don't know if he's trying to set me up or remind me who holds the power. Who asks something like that when livelihoods are on the line? I need this job, so of course I enjoy working here. Even if I didn't, I'm not about to sit in this chair and act like rent money and health insurance are optional. *Shit.*

"Yes," I say carefully.

"Are you aware that we take workplace plagiarism and professional disputes very seriously here?"

I blink. "I mean... I would hope so," I say. "Do you?"

He studies me for a moment. Then he nods.

"We do," he says. "And I'll be honest with you. I took a chance when I hired you."

Based on the way he says it, this conversation suddenly feels like it's tilting away from me, and the verdict isn't in my favor. My gaze drops to my hands in disappointment. Transparency or not, it feels like I'm already paying the price for something I did not do.

"And it paid off," he adds.

I look up, confused, not really understanding what is happening here.

"So... I'm not fired?" I ask, and I hate that my voice slips just enough to show how close I was to bracing for impact.

Ben smiles like he's been holding that card the entire time.

"No, of course not."

The relief hits me so fast it almost knocks the air out of my chest. For half a second, I feel lightheaded, like I stood up too quickly after holding my breath for too long.

Ben stands up and extends his hand. "Congratulations, Ms. Ali. *A SPARK Through Time* has been selected as our flagship SPARK concept for this year."

My brain almost blanks out in shock.

"Wait," I say, blinking fast. "What?" "Are you serious?"

"Excellent work," he continues. "Leadership was impressed with what you were able to come up with. Very strategic thinking. It's different than what we usually do, but we feel it's exactly what we need."

I shake his hand, still trying to process what just happened.

"Oh, and Lucas has been formally reprimanded," Ben adds casually. "Once confronted with evidence, he admitted to reviewing your notes without permission and using some of your ideas in his presentation. He'll be demoted to a junior, effective immediately."

My mouth opens before I can stop it. I have officially been exonerated. I can now rest my case and my worries.

"Oh, and you," he says, smiling now, "you will be promoted to Senior."

For a moment, I forget how to speak. "Oh, my goodness," I finally breathe, the words falling out of me like a prayer.

"You've earned it," he says. "There will be a pay adjustment and a bonus tied to the SPARK selection. HR will follow up with the paperwork."

I leave his office floating and feeling untouchable, completely on cloud nine without ever lighting a thing. If somebody told me I just hit a J, I would believe them. The reality is, I'm completely sober and earned every bit of this feeling.

The hallway feels different on the way back to my cubicle, like it knows exactly what happened and decided to fall in line. The floor turns into my runway, and I proudly walk my walk as I head toward my desk. I can almost hear Grandma Jamila in my head, and all her words of wisdom. This is vindication. I smile all the way to my cubicle, and then I stop cold at the edge of the cubicle partition when I notice something.

There's a cup of coffee sitting neatly beside my keyboard. A croissant wrapped in parchment paper. I didn't order it. I didn't ask for it. For a split second, I wonder who left it and whether trusting free food in this building is how people end up on a true crime podcast. And then I see the folded note. I slowly step closer, like I might startle it, then pick it up to read it.

Congratulations, Ms. Ali.
I knew you could do it.
Everything you need is already in you.
You are amazing and brilliant.
Enjoy the coffee and croissant.
--D

The smallest things always have the biggest impact on me. It's wild how something so simple can feel so big when you're not used to it. I've never had a man move like this with me, paying attention, doing little thoughtful things just because he wanted to see me smile. It catches me completely off guard in the best way. Donovan really is full of surprises, and I don't know whether to brace myself or lean in. I pick up my phone anyway, because there's no way I'm letting this go unacknowledged.

Donovan, thank you so much. Seriously, I really, really appreciate this. But how did you even know my concept would be selected?

My team found out yesterday. I had to keep it a secret, of course. I wanted to personally let you know how proud I am of you.

I really appreciate you and how you've been there for me. I mean that. I definitely owe you.

Well, since you owe me, I already know how you can pay me back.

I smile.

Oh yeah? How?

By letting me take you on a proper date.

I blink, completely caught off guard.

A date?

Well, since you owe me, you can't say no.

I laugh quietly at my desk.

Touché.

Friday, 8 p.m. I'll pick you up.

I wait a couple of minutes to respond, just for the dramatic effect.

Yes, sir.

That's what I like to hear :)

I set my phone down and lean back in my chair, letting all the emotions wrap around me. I'm getting a promotion, more money, and a bonus, *damn.*

Through it all, Donovan has been solid. He never tried to invalidate me or collect credit that wasn't his. He stood in my corner, encouraging me, as if he already knew the ending. Since I walked into OHE & Associates, he's moved like that. And if I'm being honest, this is the kind of consistency that makes a woman lose her composure just a little. Things can get quite complex if he keeps this up.

I don't feel like I'm trespassing in my own life. The fact that Donovan recognized my capabilities before everyone else did matters more than I want to admit. He has thinking thoughts I should probably table until after business hours. He has me thinking about giving him things that I probably shouldn't be thinking about.

Friday can't come fast enough. Not because of the celebration or the win, but because I want to sit across from him somewhere outside these walls, somewhere we can stop pretending this isn't more than what we portray it to be. I want to finally let the tension exhale and maybe escalate. I'm not sure about anything, but I'm open.

But before I let myself get too far ahead and before I let the romance or the celebration take the wheel, I pull my phone back out and do the one thing that matters most. I text Grandma Jamila to tell her the news.

Grandma, I got promoted.

Promoted how?

Senior Program Manager. Plus, the presentation I was working on got selected. Oh, and they found out it was Lucas who stole from me.

There's a pause. Long enough for me to picture her rereading the message, letting it sink in.

Then my phone rings.

"So, you just send that text like this is regular news?" she says, voice loud and proud. "This is something you call to tell me, Amina."

I laugh. "I knew you'd call anyway."

She's quiet for a second, then softens. "I'm proud of you, baby. I really am. I told you, I am counting on you."

I can hear her smiling through the phone. Hearing her belief in me does something to me. It reminds me of why I'm doing everything I'm doing.

"All them nights you stayed up working. All them times in your life you doubted yourself. This didn't come out of nowhere," she continues. "You earned every bit of that, honey."

"I know," I say. And for the first time, I really believe it.

"Come straight home after work" she adds. "I'll whip up something special for you."

That's not a suggestion, that's an instruction.

So, I pack up my things, shut my laptop, and head out for the day. The train ride feels shorter than usual. Probably because I spent the entire time on the train scrolling on my phone. Once I get off at my stop, I make the short walk home. When I open the front door, the smell hits me immediately.

Shrimp étouffée.

Not the watered-down kind. The real authentic kind with the brown gravy, heavy with the butter and seasoning, clinging to the air like a promise. Grandma Jamila's dad was from Metairie, Louisiana, so many of the dishes she makes have a little Cajun flair. The smell of this étouffée grabs you by the shoulders and says, sit down and stay awhile.

"Well damn," I say, kicking my shoes off. "You didn't have to go this hard in the kitchen, Grandma."

"I absolutely did," Grandma Jamila calls from the kitchen. "You earned it. You know I'd do anything for my grandbaby."

I drop my bag and walk in, my mouth already salivating. The pot on the stove looks righteous. Shrimp fat and pink, swimming in that rich, glossy gravy. Onions cooked down soft, just how I like. The celery is chopped finely so it blends in with the sauce nicely. The jasmine rice is perfectly fluffed and waiting as if it knows it's about to be baptized in the gravy.

And then I freeze out of shock. Akil is sitting at the table.

For a second, I think I'm imagining things. I wonder if I'm dreaming. His hoodie is pulled up, hands folded in front of him like he's trying to behave, as he's just staring at me.

"Akil?" I say slowly just to make sure I'm really seeing what I'm seeing.

He looks up and smiles.

"What's good, big sis?" he affectionately says. "Yeah, you surprised to see me, I know."

I cross the room and pull him into a hug, squeezing him harder than I mean to. This is how I used to hold him when we were kids, back when his head fit right under my chin. Now, he stands at least a foot above me. I remember standing over him while my mom changed his diapers, passing wipes to me while I held his ankles, feeling completely disgusted. He used to follow me everywhere, and now, as adults, not seeing him often hurts my soul.

"What are you doing here? I ask, pulling back to look at him.

He shrugs. "Grandma said you got promoted. Figured I'd pull up to show my support."

Grandma Jamila slides plates onto the table like this reunion was scheduled weeks ago. Today has truly been full of surprises.

"Sit," she says. "Eat."

We do.

The first bite of the étouffée nearly takes me out. The gravy is silky and deep, spicy but balanced, coating the rice like they were made for one another. The shrimp is tender and buttery. This is the type of food that makes you close your eyes and just sing.

"Okay," I say. "You really showed out, Grandma."

Grandma Jamila smiles proudly.

Akil watches me for a moment, then clears his throat to speak.

"I'm proud of you, sis," he says. "For real. You always moved differently and been focused on being better, and I definitely respect that about you."

I blink, surprised by how much that means to me, coming from him.

"Thank you," I say quietly.

Akil nods, poking at his food, as if he's buying himself time. "Look, I know I ain't been around like I should've," he says. "I got some stuff I'm trying to untangle. I've been carrying the weight of things I don't always know how to put down. But I'm working on it, I swear."

Grandma Jamila doesn't interrupt. She just looks and listens.

"I'm not where I wanna be," Akil goes on. "But seeing you... seeing you makes me feel like maybe I can still get it together."

My heart aches for my baby brother and swells at the same time.

"You can," I say. "Whenever you're ready. You know I'll always be here for you."

He looks at me, eyes clear for the first time in a long time. He's not high. "I know, and I appreciate that."

Dinner ends on a good note. When Akil leaves, he hugs me again, tighter this time. After the dishes are done, I head to my room and lie back on my bed, staring at the ceiling.

What a day... what a day.

Some days don't need fireworks or a big bang to feel complete. Some days you just need your cup filled. Once your cup is filled, the day just needs to end with positivity and peace. Today, I got exactly that, in a multitude of ways. The last few weeks stretched me thin, but tonight I don't feel the weight of any of that. This feels good. I fall asleep not worrying about what's next, just grateful for where I am.

13

Right on Edge

Friday night drapes itself over Amberline Heights like silk.

This Friday doesn't announce itself; it just invites itself to the party. Streetlights flicker on one by one, throwing soft halos onto the cracked sidewalks and freshly washed cars. Music floats out of open windows. Laughter echoes and disappears from rowhouses and apartment buildings. The city feels grown tonight, like it does every weekend.

Beyoncé plays loudly in my room, that invigorating, bold sound that makes you feel powerful and feminine, even when you're still sitting in your grandmother's old house. The bass vibrates just enough to tingle into my bloodstream. Music always has a way of invoking the right emotions from me.

After a long, affirming week, I can finally let my hair down. No spark decks, no office politics, no carefully curated version of myself. Tonight, I get to be just me, Amina, from around the way. The type of lady LL Cool J was referring to in his song.

And yes, tonight is my date with Donovan.

I try to downplay it in my head, like it's just casual, and I haven't been replaying his smile or the way he says my name, a thousand times in my mind. Truth is, I'm excited to see his fine ass. There's no intellectualizing that. The man is dangerously attractive, and the way he's shown up for me only adds layers to it that I can't explain.

Still, I'm still nervous. Donovan has been steady and nothing less than supportive. A small, insecure part of me wonders if I'm bringing enough to the table for a man like him. I mean, I don't even know what we're doing or what this is. He's technically not even my man. However, I'm learning that sometimes the pursuit of love means letting yourself be chosen without questioning it. I'm not sure if Donovan is in fact choosing me, but I am open to exploring this connection more.

I step out of the shower, steam still clinging to the bathroom like it's not ready to let me go yet. I take time with my skincare, the way that Grandma and all the girlies taught me. Shea butter first, warmed in my palms, worked in my skin like a ritual. Every inch of my body gets attention because Black skin deserves it. I finish with a few spritzes of my Dubai perfume, the one I jokingly say traps men. One spray at the wrist, one behind the ear, and a few across my chest.

The dress is short, but not too short. Enough leg to suggest confidence, but enough length to leave his imagination room to wander. My makeup is minimal. It's giving Nia Long in the nineties, when beauty was effortless, and didn't need a production crew. Just face, body, and grown woman energy were all that was needed back then to catch the likes of men. There's no need for me to ever do too much when the presence of me alone is more than enough. I slip into my stilettos and look at myself in the mirror.

"You look fucking amazing," I tell my reflection quietly.

"Turn that music down," Grandma Jamila yells from the living room. "I'm watching my stories."

"Grandmaaa, don't be a hater," I yell back, smiling.

The doorbell rings. That has to be him.

Grandma gets to the door first, of course. I hear her voice through the hallway, sharp with curiosity and authority. She's damn near interrogating the man.

"Who are you and what do you want with my granddaughter?"

Donovan laughs, warm and respectful. I can hear it from my room. He's nothing less than a complete gentleman as he's conversing with Grandma Jamila.

I stop stalling and finally leave my room, no longer willing to let Donovan be cornered in conversation with Grandma Jamila while I hide upstairs. I step into the hallway, adjust my dress, and make my way down the narrow stairs.

Halfway down, the conversation between Grandma Jamila and Donovan abruptly stops. When I look up, both of them are watching me. For a brief second, I feel like Cinderella coming down the stairs to get her prince. I feel every step, every sway of fabric, every breath pulling tight at me with anticipation. Except, this is not a fairytale. This is my real life.

Donovan's eyes travel over me slowly and without apology. He isn't even pretending not to look. It's almost like he's recalibrating, realizing he underestimated exactly who he was going on a date with. Of course, he's seen me at work, and he's seen me in athletic clothes, but he's never seen me done up like this.

"These are for you," he says, handing me a bouquet of fresh flowers.

Petunias.

I feel an immense amount of joy deep down in my soul.

"Thank you, Donovan," I say, meaning every word.

I pass the flowers to Grandma. "Can you put these in a vase for me?"

She takes them, still giving that look like she's measuring his character, but there's approval there now. I can see it all on her face; she likes him.

Donovan opens the front door and walks me outside to the Tahoe with his hand on my back, guiding me in the most respectful way. He opens the passenger door and carefully helps me in. Grown energy, no rushing or fumbling, just chivalry. I look back and see Grandma Jamila watching our interaction from the door. She's smiling, and I can tell she's happy for me. This is what she wanted, though. She's been hooting and hollering for years about me finding a good man with benefits.

Donovan gets behind the wheel, and before pulling off, he turns to me.

"Amina," he says with his low and deep voice, "you look incredible tonight."

I meet his eyes. "Thank you, so do you. So... where are we going?"

"There's a jazz spot I like," he says. "Live band, real music, good food, I figured we'd go there and vibe out."

"That sounds perfect," I say with excitement.

Instead of rap, the truck fills with smooth R&B. The windows are cracked just enough to let the cool night air in. I'm almost a little surprised by how good this feels, gallivanting around town with a fine ass man.

When we pull up to the spot, he hands the keys to the valet without hesitation.

Okay. He's really outside with the big bag.

Inside, the lighting is low and honeyed. Donovan has a booth tucked in the back reserved for us. Close enough to see the band, but far enough that our conversation stays ours.

He leans back, with one arm draped along the top of the booth. "So," he says, looking at me intently, "you said you got an apartment?"

"I did," I smile. "Still in Amberline Heights. It's a new construction property."

"When do you move?"

I pull out my phone to look at the calendar.

"Two weeks."

He smiles. "Okay, I'll help you move."

I laugh. "You don't have to do that," I say.

"I know." He meets my eyes, "I want to, though."

I'll be honest, I was a little on edge at first. First dates always do that to me, especially with someone I already care about more than I'm ready to admit. I kept wondering how the night would go, if the chemistry would hold on once we were in this situation. But to my surprise, there's no nervous energy at all.

Donovan opens up about being raised by his grandparents, which I resonate with since I was raised by Grandma Jamila after my mother died. He had to learn a lot of life lessons early, the same way I did. He talks about Morehouse and his grandfather's shoe-shining business in D.C., and about learning early that a man needs his own way to provide for his family.

I listen, captivated by his story. I never realized how much we had in common. I guess that's why I always get a familiar aura from him, like a shared language, even when the stories slightly differ.

Then he stands and reaches for my hand.

"Dance with me," he says.

"I don't dance," I say, smiling from nervousness.

"I got you, I promise," he replies. "It's just like riding a bike."

Once we hit the dance floor, the band shifts the energy in the entire building. The drummer starts riding the beat a little heavier and leans into a pocket beat, the familiar go-go cadence. It feels like Backyard summers, like Chuck Brown playing somewhere down the block, and like TCB warming up the whole city. The room feels very nostalgic, like I'm fifteen at the go-go. All I need is some wings and mambo sauce, and I'll be right in my element.

My body reacts to the familiar sound like muscle memory. My shoulders roll, my hips catch the beat like they have been waiting all night to let loose. Donovan catches the beat just as easy, stepping in sync behind me. We're not touching, not yet, just moving together, vibing, letting the beat do the talking. The moment feels very organic. Like two people speaking the same language without having to explain themselves. They say music brings people together, and I think it's working.

When the band eases into a slower tempo, everything between us intensifies. Donovan steps closer, not rushing or grabbing, just closing the space between us like it was never meant to be there. His hands find my waist, firm but respectful, like he's asking permission without words. I don't move away. My body answers for me, granting him permission by leaning in and trusting the moment to hold us.

He smells intoxicating, the way a good bourbon hits your chest before it ever reaches your tongue. Like an old fashioned done right. Clean skin layered with ambered warmth, woodsy vanilla, cut by spice and heat that lingers on the tip of your tongue. I caught him off guard coming down those steps earlier, but now he's the one catching me off guard. This moment and the closeness that I didn't expect, surely has my mind wandering. His scent reaches me first, slides past my guard, and makes it to the right spot. It feels like a song I haven't played in years, the one I forgot I loved until the first note lands, and my body remembers how it made me feel. Everything about him presses inward, teasing my thoughts into places I'm not sure I'm ready to visit yet.

We sway, barely dancing now, just moving together. He's looking at me, and I'm looking at him. For a moment, the rest of the room disappears, as the presence of other people and the sound of the music slips out of focus, as if we've been pulled into a private time loop only meant for us. We're locked in on each other like cuffs at the wrist, completely unavoidable.

His eyes never leave mine, not even for a second. It's like something in his head is saying, go ahead, try to look away from her, I dare you. I don't look away either. I let the tension ride, because whatever is happening right here is loud without making a sound.

His forehead dips closer to mine. My breath trips over itself, loud in my ears like my body forgot how to play it cool. I feel him press gently into my side, grounding and anchoring me, making sure I'm still here with him in this moment. I am here baby.

Then his lips touch mine. Soft at first, like he's testing the space between us, checking if it's okay without asking. The kiss is controlled and precise, but it sends heat straight through my spine. I pull back just enough to breathe, my eyes still locked in with his.

And then, I lean in again for the kill. This time, there's no question of what I want. His lips deepen against mine, still restrained but unmissably present. It's the kind of kiss that tells me he's been thinking about this moment too. The kind that says patience doesn't mean absence of desire, it means discipline. This is only confirmation that he's been desiring me for a long time, and it isn't a mere figment of my imagination.

"I've been wanting to do that for so fucking long," he says.

I smile, breathless. "So... was it worth the wait?"

His mouth curves into a dangerous smile. "Every fucking second."

When we return to the table, I'm still riding the high from that kiss, like a good sativa strain of weed. Maybe it's that, or maybe it's the glass of Riesling I sipped earlier. Everything feels like I'm floating just a little outside my body. I settle back into the booth when the waiter appears, sliding a slice of cheesecake onto the table in front of me. A single candle flickers on top, and for a second, I just stare at it, caught completely off guard, confused at what it's for.

"Oh," I laugh, still very much dazed. "It's not my birthday."

Donovan watches me like he's memorizing my face. "So, it's a celebration still."

"For what?" I ask, even though I already know.

"For you," he says enthusiastically. "Your promotion and your win."

Then, quieter, like it's only meant for me to hear, he says, "Enjoy your cake, baby."

That word hits me so hard, you would have thought Cupid himself was posted up in the corner with a bow and bad intentions. Baby. He actually called me baby. I pretend I'm unfazed, but deep inside, it has me feeling all special and shit.

After the last bite of cheesecake, we call it a night, and I don't pretend I'm not disappointed. The date was better than I expected. I knew I liked him before, but tonight made that even more evident. This isn't just work proximity or work husband shit; this is pure chemistry.

After we leave the lounge, he drives me home. The car is quiet, except for the music and the sound of my thoughts getting out of pocket. I contemplate hopping on top of him in the driver's seat and fucking him right in the car. I don't do it, though. I don't say a word. I let the fantasy stay in my mind where it belongs.

When we pull up to Grandma Jamila's neither of us moves right away. I don't reach for the handle. He doesn't kill the engine. We just sit there as the air between us turns viscous, a charged silence thick with circumspection and bad intentions being politely ignored. He finally steps out and comes around to my side, offering his hand like it's mine to take. I take it, and we walk to the door. Our shoulders brush as his hand stays firm at the small of my back like he's guiding me and warning himself at the same time.

He stops me just short of the door, fingers brushing my wrist.

"Hold on," he says. "Let me get one last look at your gorgeous ass."

He turns me gently, hands firm on my hips, spinning me like he's entitled to the view. I feel his eyes on me, dragging over every inch of my body, committing the image of me to his memory. His jaw tightens, the muscles in his face giving away how much self-control this is costing him.

"Damn, Amina." He mumbles under his breath.

I know that look. I've seen men fold under it before. The difference is he doesn't. He stands there, breathing through it, letting the moment marinate.

Then he steps closer, close enough that my body responds before my brain can intervene. He lifts my chin just enough to look at me properly, as if he's weighing a decision with real consequences. Instead, he leans in and kisses my cheek. It feels like a thesis statement that says I could, I want to, but I'm choosing not to just yet.

That shit nearly unravels me. It's enough to tell me that the night may be over, but this thing between us is far from over.

The second I walk inside Grandma Jamila's house, I kick my shoes off and head straight to my room, moving with a deliberateness that surprises even me. I ease onto the bed instead of collapsing into it, careful, almost reverent, like I'm preserving the evidence of the night.

I don't shower. Washing the scent of him off would feel premature at this point.

His scent still clings to my skin, subtle but stubborn. Even though I didn't want it to, I know the night had to end when it did. Any longer, we would have been making love songs. Sitting in this bed feels like a quiet form of torture when I wish he were here with me.

My phone buzzes.

Can't wait to see you again, Ms. Ali.

I smile when I read his message, thumb pausing over his name like I don't already know what it does to me. Damn. I haven't felt this way about anyone since junior year in college, back when I was tangled up with my ex. When that ended, I shut that part if me down. Donovan is the first man who's cracked that door open since then, and I don't hate it nearly as much as I thought I would.

I curl onto my side and pull the covers up, keeping the memory of him right at the front of my mind. I replay the kiss once, then again, and again. Donovan is the shit. He has my full, undivided attention. If he's the lieutenant, then I'm the private, and tonight I would've followed orders without asking questions. I think about the amazing night we had.

And then, I think about Black women all over America, stretched across highways and byways, carrying ambition, history, grief, and beauty all in the same breath. We deserve nights like this. Nights where a good Black man shows up right, takes his time, and treats us like we're worth something.

"Hey Siri, play *Happy Feelings* by Maze and Frankie Beverly."

14

Something About Him

Today is my first day back at work after that date with Donovan, and I already know this is going to be one of those days where I have to actively keep my thoughts in check. How exactly am I supposed to see him and pretend I'm not still thinking about that kiss? How am I supposed to not think about the way his hands felt so right resting on my waist? All I can do is think about the way he looked at me, like he was trying not to rush something he wanted badly.

I adjust my bag on my shoulder as I walk toward the office, trying to shake it off. We work together. Different teams, sure, but still. I don't need to be the woman who can't separate business from pleasure. I don't even know what this is yet. We haven't labeled it. Neither of us said it would be anything. Maybe it's something, or maybe it's just a good time. Either way, I can't let this make me spiral out of focus.

We have an all-hands meeting in ten minutes, so I head straight to the conference room after dropping my bags at my desk. A few people are already there, scrolling on their phones, whispering to each other. More bodies filter in as the minutes tick closer to the start time. Then Donovan walks in.

He takes a seat on the other side of the room. He's casual and composed as always, like he didn't have his lips on mine two nights ago. Our eyes meet for half a second, and he winks. I subconsciously bite my bottom lip, and once I realize what I'm doing, I look away fast, pretending to check my phone. My heart is beating way too fast for an average Monday morning.

A few minutes later, Ben walks in looking extra cheerful, a box of cookies tucked under his arm like he's Santa in business casual. He starts handing them out to the room, cracking jokes, spreading that particular kind of good mood that only shows up when leadership is pleased. The energy in the room lightens immediately. Once everyone's settled and the cookies are claimed, Ben clears his throat, steps to the front of the room, and officially starts the meeting.

"So, welcome everyone. I'm glad we could all be here today."

He runs through updates, milestones, and deliverables; the normal corporate stuff, then he looks up and looks at me.

"Amina Ali, could you please stand?"

I hesitate for a fraction of a second, then push my chair back and stand up.

"I want everyone to give Ms. Ali a warm round of applause," Ben says, smiling, "because her concept, *A SPARK Through Time*, has officially been selected as this year's SPARK flagship event."

For a split second, it feels like I'm standing under a spotlight at *Showtime at the Apollo*, where the room is deciding whether to rock with you or send you home. Then the applause hits. Not the polite and dainty kind, but the real claps that carry weight. I see everyone's faces light up and heads nod. I catch smiles that feel earned, curiosity that feels respectful, and surprise that feels a little overdue. Across the room, I see Donovan watching me, his expression slow and assured, like he never doubted this outcome for a second. It's almost as if he's been waiting for everyone else to catch up to what he already knew.

The meeting continues, but my mind stays suspended in the moment. When it ends, people stop me in the hallway. People who have never said more than two words to me are suddenly very conversational. This is the shit that makes me laugh internally.

"Congrats, Amina"

"Can't wait to see what you came up with."

"This is big, rookie."

Then Anna approaches me.

"Hey," she says. "I just wanted to say congratulations. I'm really excited to see how everything turns out at SPARK."

I study her face, searching for anything off, but it's not there. She's actually being sincere.

"Do you really mean that?" I ask.

She laughs. "Yes. Of course. Why wouldn't I?"

I shrug. "You've said some... some interesting things to me in the past."

She nods, owning it. "I know, and I'm sorry. I'm just a white girl from a small town in Mississippi. I didn't grow up around much diversity, and sometimes I speak before I think. I never meant to offend you."

She pauses. "I want us to win together and have a good working relationship."

My demeanor softens.

"Thank you, Anna."

“Let’s do lunch soon,” she adds cheerfully. “I made casserole.”

I watch her walk away, a small smile tugging at my mouth. You know what, she’s actually kind of cool. Maybe this place doesn’t have to feel like a warzone all the time. Not every day needs to feel like I’m dodging landmines, choosing my words like weapons, and staying alert just to make it through the day without catching friendly fire.

Then I hear a voice I know all too well.

“What’s up, superstar?”

Donovan is standing there with his hands in his pockets, his slacks sitting low and perfect on his hips, like they were designed specifically to distract women trying to focus on work.

“Stop,” I laugh, giving his shoulder a light punch. “You’re annoying.”

“Can I get your autograph?” he jokes.

“Oh, so you’ve got jokes, today I see.”

He chuckles. “I’ll text you in a minute.”

Back at my desk, I work like I’m in my own little world, tuned out from everything except what’s in front of me. Headphones in, female rap blasting through my headphones. This type of vibe right here makes you feel powerful without even realizing it. I’m so locked in, riding on a high of confidence. For once, the office fades into the background, and I let myself feel good right where I am.

My phone buzzes.

So, I have to be honest here.

Okay…

I can't stop thinking about our date.

I bite my lip.

I'd be lying if I said I hadn't been thinking about it, too.

Good. I've got a meeting to prep for, so I'll hit you up later.

Good luck with that.

I smile at my screen, then shake it off. I'm a Senior Program Manager now, and I have real work to do. I need the final numbers for some accounts. Virtual invitations need approval. I head over to Anna's desk for assistance.

"Hey, can you help me with these invitations?"

"Of course," she says cheerfully. "Email me the deets."

Before I leave, my curiosity gets the best of me.

"By the way... I haven't seen Lucas in a few days. Does he still work here?"

She hesitates. "Yeah. He took a short leave of absence from my understanding. I'm not sure why, though."

"Ah," I nod. "Just curious."

Back at my desk, I manage to get some work done, but my focus starts slipping the minute my mind drifts to the apartment I'll be moving into soon. I open a new tab on my browser and start browsing furniture, mentally ranking priorities. I can sleep on an air mattress for a while; that doesn't bother me. What I'm not about to do is have people come over with nowhere to sit. I don't want people to awkwardly perch on the floor like we're still in college. The living room seems like a good place to start.

I click through a few listings and realize a couple of the couches I like are at stores near Grandma Jamila's house in Amberline Heights. Part of me wants to go look today, get it done, check something off the list. However, furniture shopping feels like one of those things you don't really want to do alone, especially not for your first place. I lean back in my chair, pondering, already knowing exactly who I'd like to have with me.

I hesitate, then text Donovan.

Are you doing anything after work?

An hour passes. I'm sure he's just busy with work. Then he finally responds.

Not a thing. What's up?

I'm furniture shopping for my apartment. Want to come look at a couple of couches with me?

Are you asking me on a furniture-shopping date?

I guess I am.

I'm down. Meet me out front after work. I'll scoop you.

When quitting time finally hits, I pack up my things, shut my laptop down, and head outside to meet Donovan, fully ready for my little escapade. I'm about to gallivant through Amberline Heights with a fine man in a black Tahoe, and I'm not even pretending this is just about furniture anymore.

"Your Uber is here," he yells out the window of the Tahoe, laughing.

We drive to the store. When he steps out, he casually takes off his button-up like he's done it a thousand times. Underneath is a fitted white undershirt that hugs him in a way that feels almost disrespectful, stretched tight across a chest and arms that look like the result of at least hundreds of pushups a day and zero excuses. Every muscle is defined without him even trying, and his skin is warm and brown, like chocolate left in the sun too long. Donovan has the kind of body that stops your brain before it finishes the sentence and tells you to get it together.

He catches me staring and laughs.

"Something catch your eye?"

I hesitate, feeling my face warm up from embarrassment. "I was just...uh... distracted for a second."

He laughs in a way that is so sexy. "Take your blazer off. Get comfortable," he says. He reaches into the backseat and hands me a hoodie, and the moment I put it on and pull it over my head, I couldn't help but smile. The hoodie swallows me whole, sleeves too long, but fabric heavy with his scent. I don't mind wearing it at all. In fact, I like it more than I probably should. It brings me right back to the way his lips felt against mine.

Inside the store, he catches me off guard. The composed, buttoned-up man from work disappears, replaced by someone playful, hopping onto couches like a kid who just discovered furniture for the first time. He drops down hard on one, then another, bouncing a little just to test it, grinning when it squeaks. I laugh so hard my stomach hurts. There's something about seeing this side of him, playful and unfiltered. It brings me back to the time we went jogging.

"This one's comfy," he announces, bouncing again. "You trying to sink into it or actually sit?"

I slide beside him and immediately sink into the couch, the cushion hugging me like it already knows my habits. Soft in all the right places, but sturdy enough to hold a full day of absolutely nothing. I can already see myself posted up right here, legs tucked under me, chick flicks playing back-to-back, a pint of ice cream sweating in my hand while I pretend I'm only watching one movie. It's dangerously comfortable, the type of couch that makes you cancel plans and never look back. I'm sold before I even sit all the way back up.

"This is the one," I say, already knowing.

He nods in agreement, like he knew I'd decide that. "Good choice."

I place the order on the spot without further thought. There's no need for me to continue my search. It feels right, and I trust that feeling. When the store manager confirms delivery, Donovan immediately adds, "I'll be there on move-in day."

I look at him, half smiling, half serious. "You don't have to."

He lets out a little chuckle, shaking his head. "Woman, you are always trying to tell me what I don't have to do." His voice softens just a little as he meets my eyes. "Just sit back and let me look out for you."

Back in the truck, we're just joking around and teasing each other. Laughing about how serious couch shopping somehow turned into a whole comedy show. He taps the steering wheel to the music, glancing over at me, and I can tell he's enjoying this just as much as I am.

When we pull up to Grandma Jamila's, we both just look at each other. When I finally reach for the door, his fingers wrap around my hand, stopping me. The touch is slow and intentional, like he wants me to feel every second of it. He lifts my hand, bringing it to his mouth, and presses a kiss to my knuckles that lingers long enough to make my toes quiver.

"I'm really enjoying getting to know you better and spending time with you," he says quietly, eyes on mine.

The way it rolls off his tongue hits me like a slow jam at the cookout. His voice stays low, and his eyes don't move, like he's already decided patience is the play and whatever he's offering will still be there when I'm ready to take it. It feels like an invitation, carefully placed between us, something unspoken but very real, and I can tell he's watching closely, waiting to see if I'll lean in or pull back.

I step out of the truck, his hoodie still wrapped around me, and his presence clinging just as tightly. Before I shut the door, I glance back at him, catching his eyes one last time and letting a slow, knowing smile present itself across my lips. This lets him know that I heard him, felt him, and share the same sentiment. Then I turn and walk toward the door, carrying the promise of everything we haven't done yet. I don't look back, because I don't need to. The night already feels unfinished, and so do we.

15

What's Done in the Dark

A few days have passed since the furniture shopping escapade, and here I am again at OHE & Associates trying to act like I didn't spend an entire afternoon wrapped in Donovan's hoodie, laughing too loud, and imagining what it would feel like to have him in my space for real. I fail miserably, because that's all I can think about. My body remembers all the feelings he gives me.

The office is still painfully boring and committed to routine, almost like it gets paid overtime for it. Nothing ever changes or becomes more exciting. Sometimes, I just want a little razzle dazzle in my life. Meanwhile, my body is carrying secrets that do not match the setting at all. Things between Donovan and I seem rather... intense, and it's impossible to ignore. Every time I'm in his presence, I feel like there is an undercurrent running beneath my skin. No matter how many other conversations fill the room, none of them really matter to me. My awareness keeps pulling me back to him, to the quiet tension we're carrying, and to the way the smallest moments feel loaded with meaning. In a room full of people, he's the only one who truly feels present to me, and that alone makes everything feel a little dangerous.

Our paths keep crossing in the office in ways that look innocent on paper but feel anything but. Passing in the hallways, close enough to feel the heat of his presence without ever touching. Catching his eye across conference tables, looking at each other long before professionalism kicks back in. Casual run-ins by the coffee machine, our shoulders nearly brushing. Conversations kept short and professional, while everything I'm feeling is anything but. We pretend it's nothing, but every glance feels intentional, and every almost touch feels electric. When he smiles at me, it feels like a secret that is just for us.

I keep my head down as much as I can, headphones on, fingers moving, work flowing like muscle memory. I'm just trying to stay focused, minding my business, doing exactly what I'm paid to do, which is probably why Anna's warning catches me off guard.

I head to the break room to grab a quick snack out of my lunch box, just something small to hold me over until I can actually sit down and take a proper lunch later. As I'm rummaging through my bag, I notice Anna already in there, leaning against the counter, scrolling on her phone. She looks up when she sees me and smiles. There's some hesitance in her body language, as if she's been deciding whether or not to say something. She moves closer, lowering her voice without making a scene out of it, and that's when she speaks.

"Hey," she says gently. "I just wanted to give you a heads up."

I glance over, genuinely confused. "About what?"

She hesitates, choosing her words carefully. "Some people are... let's just say, not thrilled about how fast you moved up."

I look around in confusion. "Moved up?"

She nods. "The promotion. SPARK. All of it. You know how this place can be."

I let out a slow sigh. "So, what, they think I skipped steps?"

She shrugs. "Something like that. They're just jealous. I don't agree with them, obviously, because I know you earned it. I just wanted you to know people are watching. Not in a bad way necessarily, just paying attention."

I nod, absorbing what she's telling me. "Thanks for the heads up, Anna."

She gives me a small smile. "Just keep doing what you're doing, and it shouldn't be a problem."

I head back to my desk and sit there with this newfound information for a while. I'm not even surprised. I've been an overachiever my entire life, and this wouldn't be the first time some people got a little jealous of my achievements. People always have opinions when you don't struggle the way they expect you to.

A few minutes later, I feel a familiar presence. I glance up, and there's Donovan, posted at the edge of my cubicle, as if it's the most natural thing in the world. He doesn't pull up a chair or make a big show of it. He just leans against the partition, relaxed on the outside, hands easy at his sides, but his eyes tell a different story.

"You good?" he asks quietly.

I look up at him. "Yeah, just got a little office tea."

He tilts his head slightly, studying my face like he's already piecing things together.

"The lukewarm, someone's hating on you type of tea?"

"That exact flavor," I say, rolling my eyes. "Apparently, some of our colleagues are feeling some type of way about my promotion and my SPARK concept being selected."

He exhales; clearly, he's not surprised. "I figured that could happen." He glances around the office, then he leans in just enough to be sure that only I could hear him. "Listen, optics matter, you already know that, especially now."

I nod. "I do."

"But don't get it twisted," he says, eyes locking into mine with an intensity that makes my stomach flip. "That little bit of office tea isn't about to make me back away from you. I'm not built like that. We're not doing anything wrong. We're just getting to know each other, professionally and... personally."

Something about the way he says *we* feels dangerously good.

"Yeah, you're right, we're not doing anything wrong, I don't think," I say softly.

He holds my gaze, like he's trying to convince himself that this is normal. Maybe we're both trying to convince ourselves that this is normal. I think we're both fooling ourselves at this point.

And then, suddenly, the power goes off. Not gradually, but all at once, like someone flipped a switch on the entire building. One second, the office is alive with screens and movement, and the next it's consumed with darkness. Monitors go dead, and the office is surrounded by total darkness. A startled curse word echoes from somewhere down the hall, followed by a nervous laugh and someone asking if this is a drill. I can still feel Donovan's presence, and my heart rate starts to increase.

Before I can do anything, I feel Donovan step closer.

"You, okay?" he whispers, his voice right by my ear, deep and intimate in a way that sends a shiver down my spine.

"Yes," I whisper back.

The darkness changes everything. There are no eyes to see what we're doing. There are no walls to stop anything from happening. In this moment, there are no rules staring us in the face.

His hands find my waist, careful at first, like he's giving me time to decide. I don't pull away. I turn toward him instead, my fingers catching in the fabric of his shirt. I feel his breath on my neck, and I can feel the solid heat of him pressed close enough to make my thoughts scatter.

"Amina," he mumbles under his breath.

"I'm right here," I whisper.

That's all it takes for his mouth to find mine. This time, the restraint is gone. The kiss is electrical, the kind that makes the world tilt slightly off its axis. It feels almost magical, like heat and gravity colliding. The moment that has been quietly building between us is beginning to explode. My back quietly presses into the cubicle, and I can feel him pushing up on me closer, his body angled protectively and possessively, shutting out everything else. His hand moves along my side with slow confidence. My fingers glide over his chest, and suddenly we're breathing harder, closer, caught in a kiss that feels less like a choice and more like an inevitability.

The kiss deepens fast, no longer careful, no longer measured, charged with everything we've been pretending not to want. His hand slides lower, bold now, gripping me firmly like he's done asking for permission, pulling me close, until there's no space left to misunderstand. It sends a jolt straight to my toes, and my toes are practically curling in my kitten heels. I gasp into his mouth without meaning to. He presses his lips to my neck, and I can feel him slowly tasting me, like he's been waiting to do exactly this, like this is where his hands and his lips were always meant to land.

And then... the lights come back on.

We spring apart like we've been caught, but we haven't. My heart is racing so hard it feels like it might give me away. My lips tingle. I'm feeling feral. I can still feel his hand on me even though it's gone, the ghost of it lingering like a promise that didn't get to finish its sentence.

Laughter ripples through the office. I guess the construction outside must have temporarily caused a short power outage.

Donovan quickly gathers himself. He runs his tongue across his lips once, unhurried, eyes cutting back to mine with a look that makes it painfully clear he wants to give me all of it right now. When I say now, I mean right now. Two minutes of darkness was all it took to show exactly how far this could've gone, and the way he's looking at me says he's still very much standing in that moment.

He turns and walks back toward his desk, so casually, like the entire office didn't almost disappear for us just seconds ago. Like his hand wasn't just on me in a way I certainly won't forget anytime soon.

I stand there frozen for a moment, my breath uneven, and thoughts scattered. I'm still trying to process the fact that what happened, happened. I'm not even a little mad about it. If anything, I'm shocked by how hard it is to sit still now, and how much effort it takes not to follow him back to his desk to close that distance again. All the lines we crossed are vibrating between us, and I have a feeling it's only a matter of time before one of us stops pretending that we don't want to cross more lines.

16

I Got the Keys

Today is the day every young woman dreams of. It's the day I get the keys to my very first apartment. No roommates like back in college, no sharing a bathroom, no negotiating fridge space, and no damn nieces and nephews touching my shit. It's something that feels incredibly grown about having your own place.

"Grandma... Grandma."

I knock on her door, then ease it open without waiting for an answer. Grandma Jamila is already popped up in bed, glasses on, TV loud enough to wake the dead. Some woman on the screen is crying over a man who's clearly not worth the mascara.

"Grandma," I say, leaning against the doorframe.

She doesn't look away from the TV. "What is it now?"

"Well, today's the day I get the keys to my apartment. I'm about to head out soon to get things situated over there."

She finally turns toward me. "Alright, who's helping you though? You know you don't need to be doing all that moving by yourself."

"No, no," I say quickly. "Donovan, the guy you met... my uh, coworker, he's helping me."

She makes that little hum sound in the back of her throat. "Mmh-mm. And what else is he helping you with?"

"Grandmaaa," I say, dragging her name out. "Please, he's just being nice."

She smirks. "What's the name of the complex you moving to again?"

"The Opal at Amberline Heights."

She nods slowly. "Ok, you be safe then. Let me know when you make it there."

I throw together a small suitcase. Clothes for the week, toiletries, chargers, a bonnet, my good pajamas, and some of the essentials for starting over. I take my time, letting the room look back at me one last time, even though I'm only going up the street. Grandma Jamila's house has always been my landing pad, my safety net, and my everything for longer than I want to admit. This room watched me grow up over the years. This room has been here through long nights and many highs and lows.

I sit on the edge of the bed, elbows on my knees as I look around. I can't believe I really made it out of here. This is what I've always wanted.

I call a rideshare and drag my suitcase to the door, Grandma yelling behind me to text her when I get there, and to not let any man play in my face. I'm not sure what made her say that, but little does she know. I would never let a man play in my face.

The ride to the Opal is humbling. I watch the neighborhood with appreciation through the window. It may have been rough at times, but I'm blessed to have been able to grow up here. In so many ways, it's made me who I am today. The carryouts with the faded menus taped to the glass, the corner stores with people posted up outside, hell, the people in general, they'll all make this place feel like home. Even though I'm leaving Grandma Jamila's house, I'm not leaving my roots just yet. I'm blessed to be able to still call Amberline Heights home, at the Opal. I'll be close enough to feel safe, but far enough to feel grown.

When the car pulls up to the complex, I don't hesitate to get out. I grab my bags and hop out like I've been waiting for this moment my whole life because technically, I have. Opal at Amberline Heights is waiting for me, just as much as I've been waiting for it. The train station is a two-minute walk away, and the bus station is across the street, so it's perfect, location-wise. I love that it's in the cut, but still very much in the mix. It's planted right in the middle of Amberline Heights, where it's accessible to everything I need. The place looks as good as it sounds.

I walk into the leasing office, trying not to grin like a kid on Christmas morning. The leasing agent smiles, like she already knows what this moment feels like. She slides papers across the desk and explains everything, but I'm too busy being caught up in my own little world. It's hard to believe that I really live here now. When she finally hands me the keys, my stomach drops, not from nerves, but from anticipation. I thank her, probably too many times, and walk out clutching my keys like she might change her mind.

Second floor. Unit 212. Building 3.

Every step up the stairs feels ceremonial. I unlock the door, push it open, and step inside. The empty apartment echoes. I drop my suitcase by the door and do a slow walk-through like I'm giving myself a tour.

I bask in the kitchen, where I think about cooking late-night meals, in my sexy silk pajamas, drinking wine. I walk to the living room where I envision myself sitting around with my girls, maybe a man, laughing and just enjoying life. I walk to the bedroom where I'll sleep alone, and wake up alone, at least for now.

I stand in the middle of the apartment and laugh softly to myself. Not because anything is funny, but from being overwhelmed with joy. I really made this shit happen for myself.

My phone buzzes.

How's it looking? I'm here.

I smile in excitement because... he's here.

Come up. Unit 212. Building 3.

A few minutes later, there's a knock. I open the door, and there he is. Basketball shorts, Jordans, and a black hoodie. He's dressed so casually, but he's still fine as hell. It should be a crime to be as fine as he is.

He pulls me into him the second the door closes. His arms wrap around me, firm and sure, like he's claiming space on my body that he's already familiar with. The hug presses my cheek into his chest, and makes my body relax before my brain can slow my body's reaction down. He smells good, masculine and warm. The hug lingers long enough to make my thoughts scatter. Suddenly, moving items into this apartment feels like the last thing I want to do.

"Damn," he mumbles near my ear. "You smell good."

I smile into his shoulder, letting myself enjoy it for half a second longer before I pull back. My body feels electric now, like that touch flipped a switch I've been pretending isn't there.

"So," he says, stepping inside and taking in the space, with eyes moving slowly as he looks around. "This place is pretty nice. I see you."

I give him a tour, narrating like I've been here longer than ten minutes, playing it cool even though my heart is still doing a little two-step from the hug.

"This is the kitchen," I say, gesturing at the kitchen space. "I plan on doing my chef thing here." Then I lead him toward the bedroom, stopping at the doorway. "And this is the bedroom, where no magic will be happening."

He lifts an eyebrow, trying not to let out a smile. "I'm going to keep my comments to myself," he says, as he laughs.

Before I can fire back, my phone buzzes again. It's Heights Furniture Depot.

Ms. Ali, our driver is five minutes away.

"Hey, looks like the driver is almost here with the couch," I say.

We head downstairs, and I notice an amicable figure wandering through the parking lot, moving like he knows the area, but not the exact destination. Hoodie a size too small, hands shoved in his pockets, blunt behind his ear, moving with that careless confidence that only comes from not giving a damn. That is unmistakably Akil energy for sure.

I know this is Grandma Jamila's doing. That woman definitely sent him here, probably to spy on me, which explains why she was pressing me about which complex I was moving into. The crazy part is, I haven't seen much of Akil in months, and now suddenly he's popping up everywhere. I'm not even mad about it, because he's my brother and I love him, but showing up unannounced like a neighborhood security detail is wild.

"Akil!" I yell across the parking lot.

"Sis!" he yells back, spotting me and breaking into a jog.

"What are you doing here?"

"Grandma said you was moving and needed help," he says, like that answers every possible follow-up question.

Of course she did.

I let out a slow breath. "You couldn't just text me first?"

He laughs, "I'm not going to lie, I wanted to be nosey myself. She said some dude was helping you, so I wanted to make sure my big sis was in good hands."

"Oh... I guess," I say.

I introduce him to Donovan. They dap each other up and do that man-to-man silent sizing each other up shit. It's awkward, but respectful. Then, the delivery truck pulls up and shifts the entire family reunion moment into action.

Donovan naturally takes the lead and control. He doesn't bark orders, but guides the moment with ease, telling Akil where to grip and how to lift so nobody throws their back out on day one. The couch is heavier than it looks, awkward in a way that demands coordination. By the time they're halfway across the parking lot, the sun has started doing its thing. Donovan stops and takes off his hoodie, then his shirt, explaining casually that he's hot, like this isn't about to derail my entire focus.

Underneath, a white beater clings to him like it knows its assignment, stretched snug over muscle that looks like it was crafted by God himself. Every time this man exposes some skin, it does something to me. His arms flex as he adjusts his grip, veins raised, and skin kissed with sweat from the effort. The sight of him like this, unguarded and fully in his body, sends quite the thrill through my body that I pretend not to notice. I move closer under the excuse of helping, but really, I'm just taking a second to appreciate how good he looks doing something as simple as moving furniture. It's almost as if labor bends in his favor.

"Y'all need help? I ask sweetly.

Akil looks at me like I've lost my mind. "Sis, be serious."

Donovan smirks. "We're good, just get the door, please."

I follow them as they take the couch upstairs to my unit and set it in the living room. Akil wanders around the apartment like an unpaid inspector, opening doors, peeking into corners, nodding at everything like he's taking mental notes. I half-ignore him, while Donovan is wiping lint off the couch and wipes his hands on his shorts.

"Do you have any water?" he asks.

I laugh, a little embarrassed. "Not yet, I literally just got the keys, but the faucet works. Straight city water, but you'll survive."

He laughs and heads to the kitchen, leaning over the sink, and drinking straight from the tap, like most of us used to do when we were kids. His shoulders roll as he swallows, muscles shifting under the white beater. His broad back fills up my brand-new kitchen like it already knows him. I turn to check the cabinets, opening doors that are still empty, taking inventory of nothing, when suddenly he's right behind me.

His hands find my waist like it's the most natural thing in the world, resting on my hips all the way to the small of my back. His fingers press just enough to let me know he's present. My breath hitches before

I can stop it. It's casual on the surface, but it's loaded with passion underneath. This is the kind of touch that reminds me that we're playing a dangerous game in a brand-new space that hasn't learned our rules yet. I don't move right away, and neither does he. For a brief moment, the kitchen feels smaller because it feels as if he's taken up all the empty space.

He kisses my neck softly, barely there, like a secret meant just for me. Just enough to remind me how close we've been circling this thing without crossing it. My brother is still in the other room, so Donovan moves with care, as if he's holding back on purpose. My eyes close shut for a second, as my body leans into him.

Then I hear footsteps.

We separate instantly, like we've been caught in the act. He steps back, and I turn toward the counter. We snap out of our moment, pretending nothing happened.

Akil walks into the kitchen and stands there, squinting at us like he's trying to solve a crime. His eyes bounce between Donovan and me with zeal.

"Am I… uh… interrupting something?" he asks, dragging the words out.

"No," I say too fast, already knowing that he was in fact interrupting something.

Donovan doesn't flinch or overcorrect. He just gives Akil a calm nod like everything in the room is copacetic.

"Just helping your sister get settled," he says calmly.

Akil drags out a long, unconvinced. "Mmhmm," like he's not buying it, but enjoying the show anyway.

The rest of the afternoon unfolds in a way that feels almost perfect. The three of us pile into the Tahoe and head out to grab the last of the essentials. We ride around with the music turned up, windows cracked, and the city moving around us like a soundtrack. Akil cracks jokes nonstop, narrating his life like he's recording a podcast nobody asked for. He goes on about plans that sound half-baked but hopeful, and about ideas that haven't quite materialized yet. There's hunger in him, but there's also a lot of confusion too, like a boy trying to figure out how to become a man without a roadmap from another man.

Donovan listens more than he talks, throwing in the occasional comment, and laughing at the right moments, offering just enough guidance without stepping on Akil's pride. He's respectful and intentional as always, which I appreciate. Even when he's not touching me, I feel his presence, like he's guarding a space that belongs to us without claiming it out loud.

Once we get back to my apartment, we unload bags and boxes, moving through the rooms like this place has already started to know us. Akil flops onto the couch, spreading out like his name is on the lease, too.

"Yeah, this shit is nice," he says. "Real grown energy."

"Chill," I laugh. "You didn't contribute, baby bro."

"Emotional support counts," he says quickly.

Eventually, the sun starts to drop, and Akil checks his phone, mumbling something about needing to get across town. Donovan offers him a ride to the station, and Akil accepts. They leave, and when the door finally closes behind them, the apartment goes quiet, and I finally get to bask in the moment alone.

I twist open the cheap bottle of wine I grabbed earlier and take a sip straight from the bottle. I sit on the floor, back against the couch, legs stretched out in front of me, letting the day replay itself in fragments. From getting the keys to my place, to Donovan's hands and his restraint, all the way to the look Akil gave us. For some reason, everything feels like it's just getting started.

"Hey Siri," I say softly, my voice echoing just enough to remind me how new this place still is. "Play *New Apartment*, by Ari Lenox."

I am grateful to sit alone in the space that's entirely mine. I smile to myself, knowing this apartment is already holding secrets. One of them has Donovan's name written all over it.

17

Care Package

The last couple of weeks have been a beautiful kind of chaotic. Donovan turning my world sideways in ways I didn't technically ask for but definitely don't regret. Akil popping back into my life like a question that I'm still learning how to answer. Work pressing on me heavy but finally in a way that doesn't feel so bad. Now, finally moving into my first apartment and drinking wine in my pajamas like I always said I would. I can't even lie, I'm not mad at any of it. Not one bit.

Sometimes, I have to stop and laugh to myself because I really did this. Somehow, all the positive things have been adding up, and now they're actually paying me back with interest. Sometimes, the gratitude hits so hard, it makes me feel like I might just swoon right in the middle of my living room.

But I didn't come this far to trip at the finish line. If I get too cocky or spend too much time patting myself on the back, I might end up fumbling the bag. So, before I get too comfortable basking in the glow of my own progress and accolades, I remind myself what matters most right now. SPARK still needs to be airtight.

I've been trying to play it cool, telling myself I'm just being humble, but let's be real for a second; I'm so elated that my concept got selected. I couldn't be prouder of myself. After all the sneakiness and bullshit Lucas tried to pull, I still came out on top with clean hands, a clean conscience, and my head held high. This alone feels like a win, but it's bigger than that. I'm standing on the edge of the biggest moment of my career thus far, and I can feel it in my soul. SPARK is a little over a week away, and this isn't just another event on the calendar. This is my event in a way. This year's SPARK is a reflection of my concept, and it has my name attached all over it. I'll be damned if I don't make it the best SPARK OHE & Associates has ever put on.

I get to the office and start to work with tunnel vision. No distractions or daydreaming, I'm fully locked in, ready to give SPARK every last ounce of energy I've got. Today's main mission is the menu, and honestly, I'm excited about this one. I managed to secure one of the hottest up-and-coming chefs in Amberline Heights, Chef Dion. I've been following his social media page for a minute now, watching him post dish after dish. Everything he posts looks like it tastes better than it photographs, which is saying something when the pictures already look amazing. Being able to book him feels like a full-circle moment, and let's be clear, it's not even my money. It's OHE & Associates' budget, which has already been approved and signed off on. So really, everybody wins. A win is a win.

I'm moving through the office like Olivia Pope on a good day. Everything in the day just clicks and problems solve themselves. Typically, when I get an idea, I don't sit on it. Instead, I execute. Today, my bright idea for the menu is to have Chef Dion create a menu that reflects what the people at OHE & Associates actually love to eat. I don't want some stiff, generic corporate spread. Instead, I want a menu of food that feels familiar and personal. If SPARK is about connection, then the menu should reflect that too. I throw together a quick form, print it out, and start making my rounds. I ask colleagues to add their dish of choice so that I can get it over to Chef Dion as soon as possible.

I stop by Anna's desk first and explain the idea. She lights up immediately, like she's been waiting to be asked something that doesn't involve spreadsheets all day. Without hesitation, she writes down her choice. I'm not surprised that she chose deviled eggs. I think everyone loves deviled eggs.

I spot Lucas at his desk a few rows over. We haven't said anything to each other since everything came out, and it was officially confirmed that he stole my work. For a split second, the petty part of me considers letting that silence go on forever. But the louder part of me, the part that's grown, reminds me that I don't need to hold grudges or prove anything to him. I also don't want him thinking that little fiasco knocked me off my game. So, I straighten my shoulders and walk right up to his desk like nothing ever happened.

"Hey, Lucas."

He looks up, a little startled, then softens his demeanor. "Oh, Amina. Hey, how's it going?" His voice carries that slight edge of embarrassment, as if he's not quite sure where he stands with me.

"I'm good," I say easily. "I'm having people around the office fill out this form with their dish of choice for SPARK. I wanted to see if you wanted to add something."

He pauses, then nods. "Yeah. Thanks for asking."

He fills it out, and interestingly enough, his dish of choice is chicken fingers. It always humors me when a grown ass person is still obsessed with chicken fingers. I take the paper back, give him a polite smile, and turn to walk away when he clears his throat behind me.

"Hey, Amina," he says. "I really do apologize for what transpired."

I stop just long enough to acknowledge it. "It's okay," I say with a small smile, and then keep it moving.

The old me would've delivered a long and drawn-out lecture, broken everything down, and explained how it was wrong. The new me, though, doesn't need to do all of that. The consequences have already been handed to him. Lucas knows he messed up, and I don't need to stick the knife in further. Everybody makes mistakes; it was just unfortunate that his mistake involved me. It's even more unfortunate for him that I still came out on top.

I make my way over to Donovan's desk without even realizing I'm doing it, like my feet already know where to go before my brain can offer commentary. But when I get there, his space is empty. His chair is pushed in, his computer monitor is dark, and his typical coffee mug is not there. That alone throws me off. It's already past midday, and Donovan is usually in by now. He's usually buried in emails or in some meeting that could've been an email.

For a second, I tell myself it's none of my business why he's not here. I'm not his keeper, or his woman. But concern wins the battle between minding my business and not minding my business. Maybe I am being a little nosy, or maybe I'm just human. Either way, I pull my phone out to text him.

Hey Donovan, you good? I noticed you aren't in today.

A few minutes pass, just long enough for me to pretend I wasn't watching the screen.

Yeah, I'm sick unfortunately, so I decided to just take the day off.

My forehead creases immediately.

Oh no. What's wrong?

Sore throat, cough, runny nose. I'm literally dying lol. It must be a bad cold.

I smile; of course, he's being so dramatic as men typically are when they're sick.

Oh, I'm sorry to hear. I really hope you feel better.

Thanks. I'm about to go drown in some couch syrup.

I shake my head at the phone, equal parts amused and worried. I already know that "literally dying" probably means he's wrapped in a blanket somewhere, acting like the world is ending. Even though I don't say it out loud, a quiet thought drops in my mind. *He shouldn't be sick by himself.*

I can't lie, part of me is disappointed he's not in today, but what really gets me is knowing that he doesn't feel well. Donovan is usually a walking shot of espresso. He's always upbeat, always joking, and always holding the room together with that easy energy of his. So, hearing that he's laid up somewhere, miserable, makes me feel sort of uneasy. I hate the thought of him having a rough day, especially when he's been nothing but solid with me since day one. If anyone deserves to be taken care of, it's him. Suddenly, I want to be the one to do it.

I sit back in my chair and let my mind wander, plotting quietly like this is a personal mission because... well, it is. What would actually help him? What would he want right now? Soup feels obvious, and of course, ginger ale. And then the lightbulb comes on in my very capable, slightly mischievous brain. We have an employee recall roster. Every employee's contact information is in there, including addresses. I could discreetly take a quick look, grab his address, and show up with a little care package.

Now, I know it's risky and probably a little unethical. My brain immediately tries to sabotage me with worst-case scenarios. What if he has a woman on the low? What if he doesn't want me there? What if this crosses a line? I think about it for all of three seconds before deciding that I don't care about any of that. Sometimes you have to choose bold over right. Today, I'm choosing to be bold. I'd rather beg for forgiveness than ask for permission.

I put my head back down and give work another solid two hours, finishing up the last of the menu inputs and organizing everything so that I can send it off to Chef Dion before I leave for the day. Once that's done, I pack my bag like I'm heading home, but I already know that I'm not. Instead of taking my usual route home, I detour to a corner store not too far from Donovan's address. I don't grab anything fancy, just the sick-day essentials. Chicken noodle soup, saltine crackers, and ginger ale. I also grab some cookies, because honestly, I feel like everyone likes cookies when they're having a bad day. I even grab a simple, get well soon card. It's nothing deep, just enough to let him know that somebody thought of him.

I take everything to the counter, pay, and watch as the cashier drops it all into one of those thin brown plastic bags that always feel like they're one wrong step away from ripping. I knot the handles together, sling it carefully in my hand, and step back outside. The late afternoon air brushes against my face as I start making my way toward Donovan's place.

The walk takes about ten minutes, just long enough for my nerves to catch up with my decision to unexpectedly show up at his place. When I finally reach his house, I slow down to scope the scene. It's a small single-family home perched on a wide hill, and very modest. His Tahoe is parked in the driveway, confirming that he's home. There aren't any other cars in sight, and that eases my mind a little. I walk up the hill to the steps, and my heart is racing. I knock on the door three times, evenly spaced, like I'm tapping out some unofficial Morse code.

About thirty seconds later, the door creaks open. There he is. Donovan stands in the doorway, blinking at me like he's not quite sure I'm real. I'm staring at him. He's staring at me. We're both frozen in the moment. He has on flannel pajama pants, a white beater, and a durag tied low on his head, and yeah... he looks sick. His eyes look tired, but he's still fine as hell regardless.

"Amina," he says, surprise all over his face. "What are you doing here?"

Initially, my mind goes blank, like I forgot how words work. I recover quickly, lifting the plastic bag between us as if it's proof of good intentions. "I brought you some goods," I say, trying to sound casual even though my heart is doing laps in my chest.

His expression sweetens immediately. He takes the bag from my hand and smiles in a way that says that he's thankful without saying it. "Well," he says, stepping back to make room, "don't just stand there, come on in."

As I step inside, I look around and mentally analyze his space. The house is older, but I can tell it's been updated in certain areas. The white walls are paired with black furniture. The overall aesthetic is quite minimalistic. There are no pictures on the walls, no throw pillows, no candles, or color accents in general. It doesn't take a detective to determine that a woman definitely does not live here.

He gestures toward the couch, and we sit side by side, close but not touching. I watch him as he tears open the plastic bag as if it's holding the answers to all his problems.

"Okay," he says, as he looks inside. "What do we have here? Soup, cookies." He nods approvingly. "Yeah... I needed this for sure."

I just sit there smiling, watching him dig through the bag. He looks like a kid on Christmas morning, eyes lighting up over the simplest things. It does something to me, seeing him like this.

"Well," I shrug, trying to downplay it, "it's the least I could do."

He tilts his head, curiosity creeping in. "But what I don't understand... how did you find out where I live?

"Okay, don't be mad, but I found it in the recall roster."

He bursts out laughing, and the sound is contagious. I laugh right along with him, as the awkward tension melts away.

"I just wanted to make sure you were good," I say, reaching up without thinking and pressing my hand lightly to his forehead. "You feel a little warm."

"I do?" he asks, amused.

"Yeah," I say, already grabbing the soup from the bag. "Point me to the kitchen. I'm about to heat this up for you."

He smiles and gestures toward the back of the house. I head into the kitchen, grab a small pot from the cabinet, pour the soup in, and set it on the stove. While it heats up, I do a quick scan of his cabinets in an effort to locate the seasonings. I find the garlic powder and black pepper, and sprinkle some in the soup to doctor it up.

"Bowls are in the upper cabinet to the right," he calls out.

"Got it," I reply, as I move through the kitchen, almost as if I belong there, even if it's just for tonight.

Once the soup is fully heated, I pour it into a bowl and carry it back to the living room, careful not to spill it. I hand it to him, and he settles back against the couch, like he's been waiting for me to come over and care for him all day. We spend the next little while just talking and laughing, nothing too serious. I learn quickly that Donovan is a big ass baby when he's sick. I also find it funny how he coughs in between bites but still keeps going in for more. I don't mind any of it. I'm glad I could show up for him in this small way, since he's always shown up for me.

At some point, I catch him staring at me. Not in a flirty or sexual way, but as if he is really seeing me for who I am. It's like he's taking me in and committing the moment to memory. The look gives me butterflies, and suddenly I feel the spirit of shyness come over me, which almost never happens to me.

"Why are you looking at me like that?" I ask, dropping my gaze and smiling.

He responds eagerly. "Because... you're so fucking dope."

I press my lips together, smiling like a teenager who just got her first compliment from the cute boy she likes.

After he finishes the soup, he changes his position on the couch. "So, what are you doing Friday?" he asks. "Maybe we can link up if I'm feeling better."

I flash my eyes at him. "Well, this Friday my best friend is coming into town from Chicago, so I'll probably be tied up with her," I say.

"Ah, okay. All the way from Chicago," he says, a hint of disappointment slipping through his voice. "That'll be good though. I'm glad you get to see her."

We keep shooting the breeze for a while after that, the conversation remaining easy and unguarded. Just laughter, random stories, and little moments that make time move faster than it should. Before I know it, the night has crept up on us, and I glance at the clock, realizing I stayed later than I intended to.

"Hey," I say, as I stand up. "Can I use your restroom before I head out?"

"Yeah, of course," he says. "Right down the hallway."

I step away to freshen up, catching my reflection in the mirror. When I head back to the living room, Donovan is still sitting on the couch, phone in hand, waiting.

"Well, D," I say softly, grabbing my purse. "I guess I'm going to head out."

He stands immediately. "I called you a ride while you were in the bathroom," he says. "I don't want you taking a train, bus, or walking too far this late."

I pause, caught off guard. "Donovan... you really are full of surprises. I appreciate the chivalry, as always."

He shrugs and laughs like it's nothing. "I'm just being me."

We step outside together because my rideshare is on the way. There is no way a man like Donovan would have me, or any woman at that, waiting outside alone. So, we stand there together waiting, close but careful, both of us aware of the invisible line we're not crossing tonight. When the ride pulls up, we turn toward each other.

We embrace each other in a hug, but it's restrained. He pulls back first, smiling. "I don't want to get you sick."

"I appreciate that," I say, even though a part of me doesn't want to let go at all.

As I slide into the backseat of the car, I turn back for one last look. He's still standing in the driveway, looking so good it makes me seriously consider telling the driver to stop, so that I can get out and run back to him. There's something about being cared for and being considered that feels good. I hope he understands how much I truly care about him. I hope he knows that I value him.

The ride home gives me time to sit with things. This was not just about soup and cough syrup, and me popping up unannounced. This was intimacy in the most subversive form. He let me see him unguarded, feverish, human. I showed up without being asked, without an exact agenda, and that reciprocity feels consequential. There is a certain gravity to being trusted in moments like that. If this is how he lets me take care of him, I can't help but imagine all the other ways he might return the favor once he decides to stop being so damn restrained.

I know he's not my man, but I'd be damned if another woman thinks she's pulling up on him with soup, a care package, or any of that shit. Donovan is already marked, whether he knows it or not. Any woman confused about that is welcome to find out.

This was foreplay in plain clothes. This is no longer casual, and I have a feeling it's only going to get harder to pretend otherwise.

18

Sister, Sister

It's 630 p.m. on Friday, and the week has finally loosened its grip on me. SPARK is temporarily out of my mind. Tonight isn't about deliverables, optics, or proving anything to anyone. Tonight is all about my girl coming home.

I straighten up my living room for the fifth time even though nothing is actually out of place. I keep checking my phone in anticipation, like Atlantis might magically teleport here if I stare at the phone hard enough. It's been too damn long since I've seen my girl. Too long since I've laughed without filtering myself, and too long since I've just been around someone who knows every version of me.

She knows corporate Amina, who sends calendar invites and talks in complete sentences. She knows hood Amina, who still side-eyes everything and will still check a motherfucker when necessary. She knows sad Amina, who lost both her parents. She knows Brown University Amina, and the Amina who used to sit on sidewalks around Amberline Heights, dreaming of better days.

Then the knock comes. Three loud, impatient knocks.

My heart jumps before my feet move.

"Mina!" Her voice cuts through the door, loud as hell and unmistakable.

That's definitely my girl. "Tee!" I shout back, already smiling ear to ear as I open the door.

We embrace in the doorway; bodies pressed so tightly together like we're trying to make up for lost time. This is a hug that holds years in it. She smells like Chicago air, perfume, and home all at once.

"I missed you so much, girl," I say, with tears almost coming out of my eyes.

She pulls back, hands still gripping my arms and eyes scanning me like she's taking inventory. Like she's making sure I'm good, for real.

Atlantis, or Tee if you really know her, is my best friend in the truest sense of the word. We've been locked in since we were seven years old, little girls with scraped knees and big opinions, running around Amberline Heights like we owned the entire neighborhood. We have the kind of friendship that is so wholesome, it grows without outgrowing and survives distance and different dreams. After we graduated from Ballou High School, life took us on different paths. I went on to Brown, and she stayed closer to home and soaked up the HBCU magic. Different campuses, different energy, but the rhythm between us never changed. We still knew when to call without saying why. We still laughed at the same dumb things. We still told each other our deepest secrets, even when they were a little embarrassing.

After undergrad, she chased the wind all the way to Chicago and challenged herself in an amazing city. I stayed on the East Coast, went to graduate school in Maryland, and buried myself in more education. Through all of it, Tee never drifted into the background. She's the person who's always been in my corner when things go right and when they fall apart. The one who remembers who I was before the accolades, before the titles, and before this new polished version of myself appeared. I know, without ever having to ask, she wants the same thing from me. Standing here with her in the doorway, I feel an immense amount of gratitude, just to have her here and to still have her in my life after all these years.

"Oh, shit, Amina girl... this is niceee," Tee says, dragging the words out as she turns in a circle, taking in the space.

I smile because it makes me feel good that she approves of it. "Thanks, sis. It really does hit different knowing this is mine."

She drops her bags by the door and kicks her shoes off like she's already decided she lives here too. I grab them before she can protest. "Get comfortable," I tell her. "I'm about to get us right with some food and wine."

I head to the kitchen and move like I've been rehearsing this moment. I pull out the oversized wine glasses I picked up from the store the other day. I pour the blueberry wine, heavy, because that's the only way wine should be poured when your best friend comes into town. When it's just almost spilling over, I slowly carry them back to the living room like offerings.

Tee takes one look at the glass and laughs. "Yeah, you did that."

She flops onto the couch, stretching out like she's testing the comfort. Why is everyone always testing my couch? "We need wings," she says immediately, like it's not even a suggestion. "Good ones."

"Say less." I grab my phone. "The usual?"

"Twenty-piece, half mambo, half garlic parm."

"Of course," I say, already typing in the order on my phone. "Blue cheese for me, ranch for you."

She rolls her eyes. "Here you go with that bougie nonsense."

"Blue cheese is sophisticated," I tell her, dead serious. "It has depth. Ranch is just basic."

She laughs, that homegrown laugh I've missed, loud like summer on Georgia Ave, filling up the room and easing something in me that I didn't know was tight. The order goes through, the wine is flowing, and just like that, the apartment feels like old times.

We drown in conversation, so easy and genuine. There's never any catching up awkwardness or warming up with us. It's always just straight back to *us*. Laughing, interrupting each other, filling in the blanks before the other can finish the sentence. Out of everything I've built, chased, or fought for in this life, my relationship with Atlantis is one of the things I hold the closest. That's not just my best friend; Tee is my sister. She knows my past but is still so rooted in my future.

We start reminiscing about growing up in Amberline Heights, back when the neighborhood had a way of raising you fast, whether you were ready or not. Tee brings up the time we got caught in the middle of a shootout, where two streets were beefing over something neither of us could even explain now. We were just kids, learning way too early how to navigate complex situations. I remind her how we walked home afterward like nothing happened, brushing off our clothes because we didn't feel like explaining to anyone that we had been that close to potentially losing our lives that day. She laughs and shakes her head, saying we were crazy.

Then she brings up the time we really thought we were grown. We skipped school, hopped on the wrong bus, only to end up in a whole different county with no plan, and barely enough money to get back to Amberline Heights. I can still picture Grandma Jamila standing in the doorway when I finally made it home, arms crossed, disappointment radiating off her like heat. That ass whooping was historic. Tee laughs so hard she almost spills her wine, reminding me how my grandma didn't even yell first. She just stared, and honestly, that made it worse.

We sit there for a moment after the laughter fades, processing the emotions. We think about all the bullshit, the close calls, and all the ways that the world tried to swallow us whole over the years. Somehow, we made it out. Somehow, we turned all the chaos into drive, discipline, degrees, and careers. Our dreams were always bigger than the blocks we grew up on. Now, we're two accomplished women, still standing, still laughing, and still choosing each other. In that moment, sitting on my couch with wings on the way and wine in my hand, I feel richer than I've ever been.

We talk about her job next, because Tee has always been about her money. She is one of the youngest assistant principals in Chicago, and every time I say that out loud, it still makes me smile at how bad ass that is. She's always loved kids and always had that mix of patience and authority that makes children listen. I tell her, like I always do, how proud I am of her, especially knowing how easily our paths could've gone left. We dodged teen pregnancy, dodged getting stuck, and dodged a lot of traps that didn't miss plenty of girls we grew up with. Somehow, we still made it to the lives we used to think about when we were little girls. Seeing her live out her purpose like this just feels like everything has come full circle.

"Amina," she says, leaning back against the couch, wine glass balanced in her hand, "Chicago is cool, but I think I'm ready to come back home." She pauses, softer now. "I miss my family. I miss you."

I don't even hesitate with my response. "Then make a plan and come back," I say. "You can crash on my couch if you need to while you figure things out. You already know that."

She laughs, shaking her head like she already knew I'd say that. "Thank you. I think I'll finish out this school year in Chicago, but I'm going to start looking now and see if there are any positions open for next school year here, in Amberline Heights."

"Do it," I say. "The Heights needs you back."

Naturally, the conversation shifts, because it always does. From careers and homecoming plans to men. If there's one universal truth, it's that women will eventually get to the topic of men, no matter how serious the earlier conversation was.

"So," I ask, dragging the word out just before the point of annoyance, "how are the men in Chicago? You talking to anybody worth keeping around?"

She rolls her eyes, dramatic as ever. "I've been dating, having fun, and living my best single life. But if I'm really going to move back to Amberline Heights, I'm probably not going to get serious with anyone here in Chicago." Then she turns the tables and flashes her eyes at me. "What about you, girl?"

I hesitate, probably a few seconds too long.

"Well... there's this guy."

Her whole body perks up. "Ohhh, spill the tea," she says, grabbing my thigh like we're back in high school again.

I laugh, already feeling exposed. "We work together," I say, too fast. "But we're cool too, like... friends." Even as the words leave my mouth, I know they sound like bullshit. "But," I add, "we kissed."

She stares at me, clocking all my bullshit. "Friends don't kiss."

That's all it takes for me to divulge everything to her. Fifteen minutes later, I've told her nearly everything about Donovan. I told her about how he showed up for me when work had me in a bad mental space. How he checks on me consistently without hovering. I told her how he listens and makes me laugh. I also told her how fine he is, in a way that feels unfair to the rest of the world. She knows about the furniture shopping escapade, the power outage freak-off, and the care package I brought him the other day. I tell her that we haven't put a title on it, that we're just spending time, and it's nothing more than that.

Tee listens without interrupting, nodding like she's cataloging every detail. When I finish, she leans back, sipping her wine, a knowing smile on her face.

"Mina," she says calmly, "you sound sprung, girl."

I open my mouth to argue, then close it, because I can't really disagree. Maybe I am a little gone. I mean, I literally showed up at this man's house unannounced.

The truth is, whatever this thing is between me and Donovan is, it has already gotten deeper and more complex than I planned for. I can't dodge myself or the truth anymore. I know better than to lie to my own face or my best friend.

Then, there's a knock at the door, and it's the delivery driver with the wings. As soon as I open the door, it smells like a U Street carryout after the club lets out. I grab the bag, tip him, and come back inside like nothing in the world could interrupt our night. Tee already has that look on her face. It's the one that means she's about to say something I don't want to hear, but probably absolutely need to hear.

"Amina," she says, leaning back, eyes sharp but loving, "you're smart as hell, but you have to stop intellectualizing desire," she says. "Stop trying to think your way out of liking somebody. You keep telling me y'all are just friends, just coworkers, just hanging out. Girl... cut the bullshit."

She points her wing at me like punctuation. "You want him, and it doesn't matter if you two work together," she continues. "You don't need permission to go after happiness. If you want some Donovan, then get you some Donovan."

I don't even try to defend myself. We just look at each other for a second, and then we lose it. Laughter from the gut spills out of us, loud and free. I down the rest of my wine without shame, and we devour the wings like they owe us money. There's mambo sauce on my fingers, and joy in my heart.

By the end of the night, we're obscenely tipsy. The music is turned all the way up, old-school R&B sliding into whatever the shuffle setting feels like blessing us with next. We hop around my apartment, barefoot, singing off-key, dancing, and carrying on like neighbors don't exist. At some point, the couch finally catches us, our limbs tangled together, laughter fading into the quiet sound of sisterhood and safety.

I drift off next to my best friend, wine still warm in my veins, Tee's words dancing in my head like a go-go beat you can't shake. Life keeps stretching me, asking for more, pulling me forward, whether I'm ready or still catching my breath. But this moment right here feels like somebody finally hit the pause button.

I don't need a friendship bracelet or a matching tattoo to know what this is. Tee lying beside me is proof enough. She's my day-one, my living archive, the woman who has seen every version of me and never once questioned my worth. This is sisterhood in the truest form. This is the sisterhood that keeps showing up, year after year, reminding me of what's most important when everything else is in motion.

I fall asleep knowing that as long as Tee is in my life, things will always be alright.

19

Almost Isn't Good Enough

Atlantis and I have been having one of those weekends that remind you why friendship matters in the first place. It has been the kind of weekend that fills your cup back up without you even realizing how empty it was. Friday night bled into wine-stained laughter, good music, and old stories circling the room until we passed the fuck out.

Saturday morning came in loud and proud, like it knew we had plans. We did brunch the right way. The spot was packed, the music was loud, and the food was disrespectfully good. Thick waffles crisped just right, soaked in butter and syrup. Mimosas kept flowing, heavy on the champagne, and light on the juice. Tee and I laughed over clinking glasses and talked through bites, like we had nowhere else to be. We never checked the time, because the entire point was for us to stay as long as we could, and let the week fall off our shoulders one mimosa at a time.

Saturday night, we went to a silent R&B party, and honestly, it was one of the dopest experiences I've had in a long time. The music lived only in our headphones; love songs and late-night hits poured straight into our ears while the room itself stayed quiet. There was no shouting, no chaos, just bodies swaying, couples locked into their own little worlds, and me and Tee vibing like nothing outside that night mattered. It was intimate in a way that people don't get to experience often. Just slow music, shared energy, and an organic good time.

Now it's Sunday, and there's a quiet sadness settling in because Tee is getting ready to head back to Chicago soon. I can already feel the change in the energy in my apartment, like it knows she won't be here laughing, talking shit, or stealing my blankets tonight. I'm going to miss my girl so much that words can't express the somberness I feel. But this weekend did exactly what it needed to do. It filled me back up. It reminded me of who I am outside of work, outside of ambition, and outside of carrying the world on my shoulders. The good thing is, now that I finally have a good job and some stability, I can save up some money to book a flight and visit Tee in Chicago. I guess distance isn't so scary when you know you can afford to close the gap occasionally.

My phone buzzes.

What's up! How's it going with your homegirl?

Hey you. It's been really good, honestly. But she's leaving today, unfortunately, so I'm a little sad. You feeling better?

I am. How about I bring you some ice cream to cheer you up?

I smile at my phone. How can a woman say no to ice cream?

Only if it's cookies and cream.

Lol. Say less. Hit me when you're ready for me to come through.

Before I can respond, Tee's voice cuts through the room.

"Amina!" she yells. "Come here so we can take a selfie. I need content."

I laugh, and dilly dally over to her, and suddenly, my living room turns into a mini photoshoot. Our phones are out, and we're switching poses. "Wait, do it again." "No, that angle was trash." Tee is dead serious, scrolling back through every shot like she's curating an art exhibit. She's always been like this, wanting to catch the moment while it's happening. In her eyes, if it doesn't get posted, it didn't happen.

Me, on the other hand, I'm barely on social media. I'll take the picture, sure, but I don't need the world in my business. I'd rather laugh through it, talk my shit off camera, and let the memory live where it actually matters. Still, I let her have her way. She finally nods at the results, satisfied, and I already know these pictures are about to hit her feed with a caption that makes it seem like our lives are a movie.

After our little photoshoot wraps up, Tee and I collapse back onto the couch like the weekend finally caught up to us. No agenda, no performative deep talk, just us stretched out, talking about nothing and everything at the same time, while we wait on her ride to take her back to the airport. When her ride finally arrives, neither of us rushes to separate. We stand there holding each other, arms wrapped tight like we're trying to compress time.

"I'll see you soon," she says, pulling back just enough to look at me.

"You will," I tell her. "I'll be coming to Chicago soon to visit."

She smiles, grabs her bag, and just like that... she's gone.

Now that she's gone, I decide to straighten up my place. You'd be surprised by how much damage two women can do in forty-eight hours. Cooking that turns into snacking, and snacking that turns into ordering carryout. Wine glasses left on every surface as evidence of a good time. Clothes scattered everywhere as a result of impromptu fashion shows that never quite make it further than the apartment. I clean my apartment like a Black Cinderella after a good weekend, erasing the proof, slowly folding clothes, washing dishes, sweeping, and vacuuming until everything looks pristine again.

Once I finish, I light an incense and a couple of candles, letting the smoke fill my apartment like it just clocked in for its shift. Instantly, the space smells like a grown woman who's ready for some fun. I take a step back and look around. My couch looks comfortable, the floors are clean, and everything is in place.

Satisfied, I grab my phone.

Ice cream?

The reply comes fast.

I thought you would never ask lol. I'll pick some up and be on my way.

I smile to myself, wondering what the night will bring. Maybe it'll bring more than dessert.

I decide to freshen up after breaking a little sweat cleaning. I step into the shower and crank the water temperature up to that almost-too-hot sweet spot, just the way I like it. Hot enough to make me quiver, but not so hot that it feels like abuse. I let the steam wrap around me while I wash my body with organic soap, taking my time unhurried and very intentional. This isn't about rushing; it's about resetting.

When I step out of the shower, my skin is warm and relaxed. I oil myself down at all the right places. Then, I lather my body down in rich body cream that leaves my skin soft enough to touch twice. For the final touch, I spray just a little perfume. I don't want to come off too loud or too desperate. It's just ice cream.

I slip into faux cashmere sweatpants and an oversized t-shirt, with nothing but my bare skin underneath. I feel sexy, but not raunchy. I stretch out on the couch. The TV is playing just loud enough to be background noise, and not a distraction. Ice cream is on the way, and so is Donovan. The wait is making me anxious, though.

Finally, the knock comes. When I open the door, Donovan stands there with two brown paper bags.

"Your ice cream man is here," he says, voice low and teasing, eyes dragging over me slow enough to make my pulse jump.

Grey sweatpants sit nicely on his hips, just enough to catch my attention and reveal things impossible not to notice. I just know he's hung like a horse. It's subtle, but it's the confirmation that makes my thoughts wander without permission. He has on a black hoodie that frames his shoulders, like he didn't try at all and still got it right. If only he knew exactly the effect his simplicity has on me. He smells incredible, too, but that's nothing new. His typical clean, warm, woodsy scent, layered with something luxurious. He carries a scent that lingers in the air and keeps calling you back long after he's gone.

"Come on inside. I'm excited to taste this special treat," I say.

He steps inside and pauses, eyes wandering around the apartment. I can tell he notices the candles and the incense.

"Damn," he says finally, smiling. Are you setting the mood for something?" he jokes.

We both laugh.

"Relax, I was just cleaning up a little."

He smirks like he doesn't fully believe me, then hands me the ice cream. "So, I picked up the ice cream from a local spot near U Street. Only the best for you."

He's so thoughtful. "Thank you."

We sit on the couch, the long way, so we're facing each other without making a big deal about it. My legs fit in between his like a perfect puzzle.

"Can I ask you something?" he says, glancing at me sideways.

"Depends," I reply jokingly.

"Why are you single?"

I laugh under my breath and shake my head. "Because men often don't live up to my expectations." They either want to compete with me or control me," I say. "And when they can't do either, they get intimidated."

He nods like he already knew that. "That's fair."

I look at him. "What about you? Why are you single?"

He exhales slowly, as if he's choosing his words carefully instead of dodging the question. "Because the women I've dated liked what I could give them," he says calmly. "But none of them ever wanted to build with me. They wanted access to me, but not the partnership aspect."

That answer is interesting.

The movie keeps playing, but it's really just background noise, because neither of us is really paying attention to it. Eventually, the room cools down enough for me to grab the large throw blanket sitting on top of the couch. I lay it over me. He asks if he can share it with me as if it's a formality, and I oblige. I maneuver the blanket so that it's spread comfortably over both of us. As the movie continues to play, we both get more comfortable in the moment. Eventually, his feet begin to rub on my thigh. My foot touches him, and as my feet move closer to him, I feel something. Clearly, he's excited.

The next thing I know, he gets up from his spot on the couch and towers over me. I look up at him, and he slowly comes down and kisses my neck, so gently. He starts off on the left side, then makes his way to the right side. I return the favor by kissing his neck. I moan because it feels so damn good.

When he kisses me, it's slow and sure. His mouth is warm and sweet, like he's been imagining this exact moment. His breath ghosts along my neck, kisses pressed there like he's learning me by feel. I tilt my head to give him room. I melt into him, fingers curling into his hoodie as his lips trail from my mouth to my jaw, then lower.

His hands slide down my side, firm now, and more confident. He pushes me back until I'm lying against the couch cushions, and he's hovering over me. The weight of him is intoxicating. His mouth moves lower, kissing along my collarbone. Then he makes his way down to my stomach as he lifts my shirt up. His hands are warm and relaxing. I know that he knows exactly what he's doing.

I tug on his hoodie, pulling him closer, my mouth finding his neck again, gently biting his skin.

"Amina..." he mumbles.

He kisses lower again, slower this time, and then suddenly he stops.

He lifts his head, his eyes dark, and his jaw is tight. His hands leave my body like touching me costs him something.

"I'm sorry," he says quietly, already reaching for his phone and his keys.

I sit up fast, heart racing, my body still quivering in every place he touched me.

"Donovan."

He shakes his head, standing now, running a hand over his face like he's trying to pull himself back together. "If I stay, I won't stop. So, I'm going to go."

He doesn't wait for me to respond. He moves swiftly to the door and rushes out without looking back.

Before I can process anything, he's gone.

I'm left on the couch, skin still hot, still flooding like he just cracked open a damn fire hydrant and then disappeared with the truck. Everything in me is still running. I don't understand why the hell he would leave, especially the way he did.

So why am I the one sitting here, soaked in confusion, among other things?

Did he not want this?

20

The Space Between Us

I'm lying here, breath still uneven, body quivering everywhere he touched me. I'm staring at the ceiling like it might explain what the hell just happened. My body hasn't caught up to his absence yet. It's still expecting him... It still wants him. My body is still wide open. He woke up the animal inside of me, then left it on the street like a stray.

My thighs press together instinctively, chasing some kind of relief, but it only reminds me of how close we were. Tee's voice replays in my head, loud and clear, telling me to stop intellectualizing desire, and to stop turning what I want into a damn thesis. And the moment I finally listen, the moment I stop thinking and start acting, he's gone. He lingers on me like a ghost.

I'm not angry, and that's the part that surprises me. Instead, I'm sexually frustrated and confused. My body still can feel the weight of him hovering over me. My neck still tingles where his mouth tasted me not long ago. I can feel exactly where his hands were, like they left fingerprints I can't see, but can definitely feel.

I turn onto my side, pulling the blanket tighter, trying to ground myself while my body is still very much awake. My phone is silent. The room smells like incense and him. My heart is racing for no reason other than that it hasn't slowed down yet from the wild ride I almost went on.

Suddenly, there's a quiet knock at my door, and I freeze.

I'm not expecting anyone. Honestly, I don't want to see anyone in this condition. My body is still feigning for unfinished business, my thoughts are scattered, and my nerves are exposed. I push myself up from the sexually charged space on the couch, legs a little unsteady, and slowly walk to the door.

I glance through the peephole to see who it is.

It's Donovan.

I gasp in confusion because he literally just left me hanging minutes ago. He just stands there like he never left. His hoodie is half on, with his keys still in his hand, as light moisture sits on his face. His eyes meet the door even though he can't see me. It's almost as if he knows I'm right here on the other side, deciding whether to let him back in. I contemplate the reality of the situation.

I start to open the door, but before I can even pull it all the way open, he starts talking. His words are fast, uneven, and maybe a little bit frantic.

"Amina, I didn't mean to leave like that," he says. "I just... I didn't want you to think I came here for one thing. I didn't want to mess this up. I didn't want you to think I..."

I don't let him finish. Instead, I just move closer, close enough that his words fall apart on their way out. Close enough that he has no choice but to stop talking, because whatever space existed between us before is gone now. We've come too far to not finish what we started.

"Donovan," I say very clearly, my voice doing what his can't right now. "I want you."

He pauses as his gaze drops to my mouth and lingers there. When he speaks, his voice is deep and unmistakably sure.

"Well then, tonight," he says, "I'm yours."

The words barely finish leaving his mouth before his hands are wrapped around my waist, guiding me back through the doorway. The door closes behind us with a soft thud, and suddenly, my back is pressed against the wall. His body is pressed against mine without any space between us. His mouth finds me again, deeper than before.

I barely have time to breathe before his large frame lifts me effortlessly. My legs instinctively wrap around his waist, and my hands wrap around his neck, as he carries me down the hall to the bedroom.

He doesn't rush. Neither of us say any words. By the time we reach the bedroom, there's no doubt left about where this is headed, only the knowledge that whatever happens next was always destined to happen.

The bedroom is dim, lit only by the faint candlelight from the living room and the glow from the city coming through the windows. He lays me down on the bed gently, hands still firm, with an energy that's a mix between urgency and patience. His eyes glance at my face, my mouth, then my hips. He watches the way my chest rises and falls in anticipation, and I can tell it turns him on.

He smiles, then leans in again, kissing me as if he's taking his time. I can tell he plans to remember this later, maybe even forever. His hands slide down my back and settle at my hips, thumbs pressing in with quiet appreciation. He's holding me there like I'm exactly where I belong. There's nothing timid about this moment right here. Every touch feels intentional. It feels like he's honoring my body as much as he wants it.

"You're beautiful," he says quietly, not as a compliment he expects me to take lightly, but as a fact that he's finally allowed himself to say out loud.

I breathe in, my hands resting at his shoulders, feeling his strength. His thumb brushes my jaw and tilts my face just enough so he can look at me fully. There's no hunger for me in his eyes that feels reckless. I can tell it's much deeper than that. It's desire, yes, but it's wrapped in care.

He kisses me again, slower this time, as he eases both of us into penetration. One hand remains in my hair, fingers gripping like he doesn't want to let go. It's slow intention, wrapped in passion. I rip his white beater off as I moan, revealing his entire naked chest. I take a second to just look at him; to appreciate the way his body tells its own story before I pull him back closer to me.

This has to be paradise. Nothing else explains how right this feels and how every inch of my body quivers, while my pulse speeds up at the same time. This is the kind of moment you don't want to rush through or overanalyze. I want to hold this moment right here and stretch it out for as long as I can. The way he looks at me, and the way his pheromones intoxicate me, send me to the moon.

After hours of pure bliss, we're lying in my bed now, sheets still tangled around us. My bedroom window sits on the side of us, and through it I can see Amberline Heights turning into itself for the night. The streetlights glow, casting long shadows across my bedroom walls. I can hear fewer and fewer cars riding by. It feels like the neighborhood is exhaling, and somehow, so am I.

Donovan is behind me, with his arms wrapped so tightly around me. One arm is wrapped around my waist, secure and steady, while the other is wrapped around my chest. I tuck myself into him without thinking or overcomplicating things, fitting into the curve of his hold as if I'm his missing puzzle piece.

His fingers move slowly at my hip, not wandering, just there to remind me that he's present. He shifts the blanket up around my shoulders, making sure I'm covered and comfortable. He's a good man.

"You good?" he asks softly, his voice deep in my ear.

"Yeah, I'm good," I say, my voice soft and relaxed. "I am a little parched, though."

He laughs softly behind me. "Alright then, I can go grab you something to drink from the kitchen."

"No, no, no," I say quickly, already shifting in the bed. I turn just enough to kiss his cheek, flirtatious and deliberate, letting my lips leave an imprint on his beautiful skin. "Let me take care of you."

He smiles harder, which exposes all his beautiful, white teeth. "Oh damn," he laughs. "It's like that I see. Yes, ma'am."

I slowly roll out of the bed, throw on my t-shirt, and head to the kitchen, still wrapped in the warmth of him. I pour two tall glasses of water and grab the package of chocolate chip cookies from the cabinet because something sweet feels right on time. When I come back to the bedroom, he's propped up against the headboard, watching me like I'm his favorite show.

"Here you go," I say, handing him a glass.

"Thank you," he says, then notices the cookies. "And you brought snacks too!" He grins, already reaching for the cookies.

We sit there on the bed, knees touching, laughing quietly over cookies and conversation. Eventually, the laughter fades into a comfortable silence, and we ease back under the covers. His arms find me again without asking.

This doesn't feel like a night that ends when the sun comes up. Wrapped in him, with the city watching us quietly from outside my window, I fall easily into the spirit of relaxation. Held like this, I can't tell where the night ends and something else begins.

21

Pleasure, Pressure, Proof

What a night.

I wake up to city birds chirping outside my window. The morning light twinkles across my bedroom floor, making the clouds outside look wonderful. My body feels loose and satisfied. For half a second, I just lay there, staring at the ceiling, smiling for no reason. That's how you know a woman was turned all the way out the night before.

Then I grab my phone.

"Oh, shit!" I frantically shout, shooting upright so fast the sheets slide right off me. I look at Donovan, still knocked out on the bed, and gently shove him to wake him up.

"Donovan... Donovan, wake up."

He opens his eyes and looks at me, groggy and confused. "What's going on?"

"It's Monday," I say. "We have to go to work."

That wakes him all the way up. He quickly sits straight up. "Oh, shit." He rubs his face, then laughs under his breath. "I have to go home and change, woman."

I start laughing too, because the alternative is to panic. There's no way we can both roll into work super late. I wonder if that would look suspicious.

He throws on his hoodie and those grey sweatpants again, moving quickly but still so sexy somehow. "I'm about to head out so I can go home and get ready," he says. "I'll probably be a little late, but I'll see you at work."

"Same," I tell him. "I need to get myself together as well."

"But before I leave," he says, as he grabs my chin and kisses me on the cheek.

That kiss was a quiet threat, sweet enough to scramble my priorities, and bold enough to explain why both of us forgot the entire concept of time for a night. I guess that explains why we will both be late to work today. He doesn't even know that he's about to live rent-free in my head all day.

He pulls back, smiling ear to ear. "I'll see you at work, beautiful."

Then he's gone, the door clicking shut behind him.

I finally pull myself together and move through my morning routine on autopilot, skipping a few steps due to the lack of time. Forcing myself to get into the shower is the hardest part. I turn the water on and let it heat up to my desired temperature. I hesitate before stepping in, not ready to rinse the night away. Then, reality wins; I can't show up to work smelling like hot sex and last night's decisions, no matter how good they both were.

I wash up, brush my teeth, refresh my hair, and twist it into a big, messy bun. Typically, I'll put on some heels, but today is not a heels type of day. The way he had my legs pinned up, I think I would be abusing myself if I wore stilettos today. I quickly slide on flats without guilt.

I don't even bother with the train this morning to get to work. I call a rideshare and let it take me straight to OHE & Associates. By the time I arrive, the office is already jumping. I'm a little anxious, because this is the first time I've been late.

***

"Stacy," I call out as I breeze past the front desk.

"Amina, good morning," she says, cheerful as ever.

I make it to my desk and immediately dive in. I quickly triage my emails and calendar. Being half an hour late doesn't sound bad on paper, but during a week like this, it feels criminal. SPARK is happening at the end of the week. Every minute counts when your name is attached to the biggest event of the year for the company. Everything has to be nearly perfect. I have to be nearly perfect.

That's when I notice that Ben has scheduled a prep meeting with everyone in the office. I get comfortable in my chair and continue diving into work. I double-check the guest list and review all the presentation documents with a critical eye. Vendor and guest confirmations are coming in. The catering, lighting, sound, and security pending items are all complete.

When it's time for the meeting, I grab my notebook and head to the conference room. A few people are already inside, just chatting. I walk to the back to find a seat where I can see everything without being seen too much. More bodies fill the room as minutes pass, the sounds from sidebar conversations rising and falling until the door opens again.

Donovan walks in.

He has on khaki pants and a polo, more casual than his typical fitted dress shirt that he wears most days. It amazes me how even when he's in a hurry, he still manages to look unfairly good. So good that he's definitely worth the glance I pretend not to give him. He catches my eye anyway, just for a second.

Ben comes in right after and calls the room to order.

"So, SPARK is finally here, team," he says, clapping his hands once. "I couldn't be prouder of the work everyone has put into making this happen. Let's walk through everything one last time to make sure we're fully squared away for Friday."

He launches the presentation into the rundown, highlighting the timeline, logistics, contingencies, and, of course, the contingencies for the contingencies. Slide after slide, detail after detail, an hour slips by before I even realize it.

I hear Ben's voice, but my focus keeps drifting. Across the room, Donovan quietly shifts in his chair. It seems that he just can't keep still. Our eyes meet, then we both quickly look away, then our eyes meet again, like we're testing boundaries.

Last night keeps running through my mind at the worst possible moments. I sit there trying to look composed, pen moving across the pages in my notebook, and nodding at all the right times, so it appears that I'm paying attention. The reality is, I'm not hearing a damn thing that Ben is saying because I'm too busy thinking about Donovan's fine ass.

My phone buzzes in my lap.

Well, we made it to work, lol.

Just in the nick of time.

You were definitely worth being late for.

I shake my head, amused and already annoyed with myself for how easily he can pull my attention.

Stop. We're at work, lol.

A few seconds go by, just long enough for me to think he's going to behave.

Okay… so what happens when we're not at work?

I stare at the screen longer than I probably should, heat creeping up my neck. Both his audacity and his boldness arouse me, right here in the conference room. The fact that he knows exactly what he's doing and is doing it anyway, annoys me.

I don't reply. Instead, I set my phone face down on my lap and force my eyes back toward Ben, nodding along like I'm fully locked on what he's saying. I can feel Donovan's eyes still on me, like he isn't even pretending to be subtle. I keep my gaze forward, jaw set, and posture professional. I keep telling myself not to feed into it, especially not right now.

Out of the corner of my eye, I catch Anna a few seats over. She's pretending to take notes, but her pen pauses mid-sentence as she glances up, then back down, then up again. Her gaze goes from Donovan to me and back like she's connecting dots in real time. When our gazes briefly meet, she lifts one brow just a fraction. It doesn't seem to be judgmental, more so that maybe she's clocked the energy between Donovan and me and filed it away in her mind. I just give her a neutral expression and lock my eyes back on Ben, trying not to make things awkward or obvious.

The meeting drags on for another half hour before Ben finally adjourns the meeting. All you hear is chairs scraping and people stretching. Someone even exhales a little too loudly. Since I've been at OHE & Associates, I can honestly say that was the longest meeting I've sat through, and judging by the collective relief in the room, I'm not alone. Everyone quickly leaves the room to reclaim their desks and sanity.

I head back to my cubicle, still trying to clear my head. I'm still trying to separate guest lists and spreadsheets from the memory of being tangled up in the sheets last night with Donovan. He sat in that meeting and looked at me as if work was just some inconvenient interruption to what we have going on. I drop into my chair, open my laptop, and pretend to focus on the task at hand.

Then there's a soft knock against the side of my cubicle wall. I look up, and it's Anna. I'm not sure what she's doing here.

"Amina, hey," she says, leaning against the partition like she's got nowhere else to be.

"Oh, hey Anna. What's up?" I say, keeping my tone light and friendly.

"Nothing serious. I was just checking on you," she says. "That meeting was... long."

I let out a short laugh. "Long doesn't even begin to explain it."

She nods in agreement. "Yeah, the prep meeting before SPARK usually is pretty long. It's kind of like the calm before the storm."

"Noted," I say, smiling.

She doesn't move right away. She just stands there with her hands folded, studying me with that curious look she gets when she's about to say something but hasn't decided how to phrase it yet. The silence becomes sort of awkward.

I laugh again, trying to cure the awkwardness. "Okay, what is it, Anna?" I ask.

She tilts her head slightly. "Well, I caught Donovan staring at you during the meeting."

I don't really know how to respond to that, without giving her inside information on what's really going on between us. "Oh," I say, with a neutral tone. "Really?"

"Yeah," she says, nodding like she's confirming her own theory. "I think he likes you."

If only she knew how thoroughly and intentionally that man explored my body last night. At this point, I think liking me barely scratches the surface. I keep my face composed, though, trying to give the impression that this is new information.

"Hmm," I say. "That's interesting."

She shrugs, amused. "That's just my two cents." Then she straightens up. "Anyway, I should get back to work."

I smile. "Yeah. Same here. See you later."

"See you," she says, already walking away.

I turn back to my screen, smiling, but also feeling as if I've just been caught red-handed. I pull out my phone to text Donovan with the news.

So… Anna thinks you like me.

There's a pause. It's just long enough for me to picture him reading the message and deciding how honest he wants to be.

That would be an accurate observation, wouldn't you say?

I shake my head at my phone.

Donovan, we could get caught.

Relax. It's not a crime for me to like you. Yes, we're colleagues, but we're not in the same chain of command. We're fine.

Maybe, but she wouldn't think that if you hadn't spent the entire meeting staring at me with bedroom eyes.

Well then… how about you come over after work so I can make it up to you.

He's so damn bold it almost irritates me. He has the kind of assertiveness that doesn't chase or beg, just states things like they're facts and lets you sit with it. I tell myself I'm not going to respond to yet another one of his messages. I tell myself that I'm focused on the work and tasks that are right in front of me. I tell myself I'm a grown woman with priorities, with SPARK breathing down on my neck and a reputation to protect.

But the longer I sit there, the louder my body gets.

My focus drifts. Every few minutes, I catch myself replaying the way he looked at me this morning and the way his hands felt caressing my body all night. I feel like I'm pacing internally, restless, needy in a way I don't usually allow myself to be. I still keep telling myself I'm not going to text him back. So instead of texting Donovan, I text the one person who knows me well enough to call my fucking bluff.

Atlantis.

Girl… it happened with Donovan.

There's a pause, but not a long one. Tee never lets suspense breathe too long.

Ok. Was it good, Girl?

It was… spectacular, honey.

The dots pop up immediately.

So, what's the problem, because knowing you, it's a problem?

I hesitate, thumbs hovering. I type something, then delete it, then type it again. I know how this sounds even before I send it.

The problem is… I think I want some more.

Her response comes back quickly.

Remember, girl. Stop intellectualizing desire. Get yours.

That one little text from Tee is enough to make me fold. I don't overthink it this time. I finally respond to Donovan's text.

Ok. I'll be over.

His reply comes almost immediately, like he'd been waiting on my response.

Go home and pack an overnight bag.

Ok.

He sure did tell me. I place my phone back on my desk and lean back into my chair. My pulse is already acting brand new. On the ride home,

I replay everything. His voice and his touch are incredibly intoxicating. Once home, I shower again. I wash my body much slower than I did this morning, letting the water do its thing while my thoughts wander where they shouldn't. I don't rush getting dressed. Instead, I move into my bedroom and lay everything out on the bed. Comfortable faux cashmere sweatpants, a fitted sweatshirt, and sneakers lined up at the foot of the mattress.

My phone buzzes on the bed.

I'm going to send a ride for you. Let me know when you're ready so that I can order it.

I smile while my towel is still gently wrapped around me.

You can send it. I'll be ready by the time it gets here.

Bet.

I put the sweatpants on, letting them sit just above my hips, then pull the sweatshirt over my head, the fabric soft against my skin. While packing my *spinnanight bag*, I make sure to pack a clean outfit for work in the morning so that I'm completely prepared, and there's no more being late for work. Before I zip my bag, I pause and take a good look at myself in the mirror. I smile at my reflection. For once, I'm letting myself enjoy the anticipation without trying to control every aspect of what happens next.

My phone buzzes again just as I sling the overnight bag over my shoulder.

Your ride is outside.

Ok, I'm headed down.

I step out of my apartment and lock the door behind me. The hallway lights up, almost as if it's cheering me on. I wonder if this is what typically goes down during the *demon time* they speak of in all the songs. I'm not nervous, but I'm anxious. Not in a bad way, but more so in a *Ginuwine, I'm so anxious type of way.*

I make it outside, and I see my ride. I slide into the backseat, and the driver already has Donovan's address populated in his navigation. As the car pulls off, the city moves past the window in a blur. The closer we get to Donovan's house, the quieter the outside world gets, and the louder my body gets. My body can sense we're getting closer, like a dog pulling up to its house. I'm feigning like I'm in withdrawal, and Donovan is the drug.

Finally, we arrive at Donovan's house. The driver pulls up right in front of his place. I step out, thank the driver, and adjust the strap of my bag on my shoulder. I slowly walk toward Donovan's front door. Before I even make it all the way up the walkway, the front door opens.

Donovan is already there waiting. He hasn't said a word yet. He just stands there looking at me as if he's been counting the minutes until

I arrived. I barely get a chance to step inside before he reaches for my bag, slipping it off my shoulder.

"I should probably apologize," he says, voice low and deep, but almost playful. "For Anna catching me staring at you earlier."

I look up at him, and we just stare at each other for a few seconds. Neither of us knows what to say in this moment. Then it hits us at the same time, and we start laughing hysterically.

"Actually," he says, "I recant my statement. I'm not sorry at all."

Before I can respond, he drops my bag and scoops me up effortlessly, like the decision was already made. I gasp, instinctively grabbing onto him as he carries me to the couch. He sets me down slowly, his body following mine as he leans over me, close enough that I can feel the heat of him without him touching me yet.

Then the kisses start.

His mouth drifts from my lips to the curve of my neck. He kisses my ear, then trails lower until my whole body feels tuned to him. Every place his lips touch, my body sends tingles all the way down my spine. And just like that, he has me back in paradise, surrendering all of me while my toes are pointed toward the ceiling.

I was just trying to get my footing in my first real job. I was just trying to prove I belonged in all the rooms I walk in and all the tables I sit at. Survival was the starting point, but lasting success was always the goal. I tried so hard to just keep my head down, but I wasn't prepared for all of this. I wasn't prepared to be on a sex extravaganza with my fine colleague and discovering how easily he could undo me. I never expected him to be the one pulling those sounds from my throat, night after night, leaving me breathless and satisfied. I keep telling myself that I should slow down, that this is reckless, but truth is, I don't want to stop. Behind locked doors, he is mine. Somewhere between the sex and the friendship, between the laughter and the lingering touches, I think I fell in love with Donovan.

For four days straight, we run it back like we can't get enough. His place one night, mine the next. Chasing the same high that gets us both there every time. Every time the door closes behind us, the world narrows down to his skin on mine. I crave him in a way that surprises me, because it feels reckless and right at the same time. The way he looks at me tells me it's a mutual feeling. It's almost like we've both crossed into something addictive, and neither of us is interested in rehab.

At work, we play it cool and keep it polished and professional, but the tension is always there. Every goodbye feels temporary. Every hello feels long overdue.

SPARK is tomorrow. This isn't just about excelling at OHE & Associates and my relations with Donovan. This isn't just about love and ambition finally meeting at the same intersection. It's about how I stopped choosing between desire and discipline, and how I earned the right to have both. It's about what happens when everything I've built collides with everything I want.

22

Definitely Earned It

Tonight is finally here.

After months of navigating the highs and lows of corporate America. After months of proving myself. After months of planning, pivoting, and trusting my instincts even when others doubted me. SPARK is finally here.

There's no office to report to today. There are no cubicles to sit at today or meetings to attend. Tonight, every single person at OHE & Associates is expected to show up appropriately dressed for the occasion, present, and on time at the event.

This year, SPARK is being held at a luxury hotel downtown. It's one of those hotels that looks like somebody's dream wedding venue before the ring ever shows up. I'd love to get married at a place like this. It has crystal chandeliers, attentive staff, and loud luxury. Chef Dion is catering the event, so I don't have to worry about the food being good. That alone is a win. Good food has a way of bringing people together and making things better, so if everything else fails, at least I know the food will be good.

Still, I have butterflies in my stomach from a mix of nervousness, anticipation, and excitement. I feel like I mixed light liquor and dark liquor at a college party. Everyone knows you can't mix liquor and expect to feel good from it. My vision and name are both quietly attached to every detail of this year's SPARK event. Because of that, Ben asked me to give a speech about the inspiration for the concept. He said it doesn't have to be long, and that I shouldn't be nervous, but that's easy for him to say. He's literally a professional at public speaking. I will be standing in front of executives, investors, partners, and people with money and opinions. These people don't clap unless they mean it.

When guests first arrive, they'll partake in a happy hour and hors d'oeuvres session. That first hour is needed because it gives all the guests time to arrive, settle in, and loosen up, especially with all the alcohol. All the liquor will be Top-Shelf, because people with money expect nothing less. After that session, the doors to the main ballroom will open, and attendees will be escorted to their tables.

Anna and I spent hours curating the seating arrangements. We balanced personalities, industries, and values, with the goal being to spark intentional conversation between attendees who are seated together. We also had to determine who should absolutely not be seated together under any circumstances. It felt less like event planning and more like matchmaking. By the time we finished, we felt like every table would create some good conversation pieces. Tonight, we get to see if our theories are correct.

Once everyone is seated, the line for food will open. My hope is that people will stand in line, mingle, laugh, and move toward the food expeditiously. Chef Dion really showed out on this menu. There will be deviled eggs topped with spiced shrimp, because Anna was adamant about her deviled eggs. There will be honey butter chicken and waffle sliders, a refined version of Lucas' very simple request for chicken fingers. Most importantly, there will be plenty of mini crab cakes, golden and perfectly brown, because that was a non-negotiable for me. Chef Dion took everyone's preferences and turned them into something unique and very appropriate for this occasion.

About an hour after that, once most people have finished devouring the food, the event will transition to the actual presentation. Ben will take the stage to deliver the presentation on behalf of OHE & Associates. He'll walk everyone through who we are, what we've built, and where we're headed as a company. Once he finishes, he'll call me up for my short speech. Even thinking about it now makes me want to pass out, knowing that I have to make a speech in front of so many important people.

I also asked Ben if it would be okay for me to bring Grandma Jamila. I need her there with me. I also want her to see the event with her own eyes, to witness what all those years of sacrifice and prayers actually produced, in terms of me. If I'm being honest, I also wanted one person in the room with me who felt like home. Someone I didn't have to perform for. Ben immediately told me yes when I asked him.

Donovan will be there too, obviously. The thing is, whatever this thing is between us, it still lives in the shadows. So tonight, we keep it professional in public and personal in private, just as we always do.

Ughhh.

My mind is everywhere all at once. Joy layered over excitement, and excitement tangled in nerves. I can feel how big tonight is, and how much it matters. I glance at the clock on my phone, and reality sets me straight. It's almost two o'clock. If I need to be walking into SPARK by five, I need to get my shit together now.

I step in the shower first, because any good hygiene routine starts with clean skin. The water hits me, sliding over my shoulders, down my back, washing away all the nervous thoughts clinging to me. I take my time with it, letting the steam soften me while my body relaxes. By the time I step out, I feel a little less anxious.

Then I turn my attention to my hair. I twisted my locs yesterday on purpose, knowing all I'd need to do today is to let them loose. I stand in front of the mirror and undo each twist slowly, one by one, letting the curls bloom and fall where they want. I run my fingers through my hair, fluffing, shaping, and admiring the way my locs frame my face when they're free.

I slip into the dress I bought weeks ago on sale, knowing it was meant for this moment. It's red and slightly form-fitting. It hugs me in all the right places, while it's both sexy and classy.

I stand in front of the mirror fully dressed, and for once, there's no critique running through my head. Just adoration for the woman looking back at me. I'm loving everything I see, and I'm loving who she has become. These past few months have allowed me to really grow and mature as a woman, which was part of the goal.

"Amina, you're a star," I say softly to my reflection, meaning every word.

A single tear slips down my cheek. Sometimes tears show up when all the emotions you've been feeling finally catch up with you. I dab it away quickly, laughing at myself because I didn't spend this much time getting ready to let my emotions ruin the moment, or my makeup. There will be time for tears later, but definitely not now.

As a gift to me for all the hard work I've put in, Ben arranged for a limo to pick me up. He said it casually, like it was nothing, but it really was a thoughtful gesture to me. I check the time and realize the driver will be here in about ten minutes.

While I wait, I walk into the kitchen, pour a small shot of rum, and knock it back. I chase it with apple juice, the mix settling my nerves just enough. I don't need to be tipsy, I just need something to take the edge off.

Right on cue, my phone buzzes.

Ms. Ali, I'm your driver, Rami. I am just letting you know that I'm outside when you're ready.

Thank you. I'll be right down.

Before I leave, I pause in front of the mirror and give myself the respect of not rushing past this moment. One more look won't hurt. I've learned not to speed through things that took years to build. This day did not come easy at all, and neither did the woman standing here in it. I adjust my dress, roll my shoulder back, lift my chin, and let the image of me settle into my mind. This is a moment I will remember forever.

What catches me off guard is how much I look like my mother right now. Not just in the face, but in the presence. My mom used to stand like this when she meant business, when she was already ten steps ahead and didn't need to explain herself. The woman looking back at me in the mirror has receipts, and the pride that fills my chest is quiet, expansive, and incontestable. I know my mom would be proud.

It's too bad she's not here with me physically, but I know she's always with me spiritually.

I head downstairs and step out front as Rami pulls up. I wave instinctively, as if this is a normal part of my life now. Rami hops out, walks around, and opens the door for me. I gently slide inside, and he tells me to sit back, relax, and enjoy the ride. I do exactly that, because this is my life, at least for tonight.

I glance around the limo and can't help but to feel like a mother-fucking boss. Leather seats, dark windows, Champagne, I tell you, I sure have come a long way from the Metro bus to a limo. For a second, I wonder if this is how Beyoncé feels on a random Friday, headed to an event. Probably not, but I'm letting myself live in the moment anyway. I get comfortable like I've been here before, even though my mind is screaming, Amina, look at you.

We cruise down 295 and, of course, traffic is acting a fool. Brake lights stack up like a petty reminder that even in a limo, you still have to wait your turn. I remain unbothered, watching the city light up outside the window. Amberline Heights is fading behind me as we inch closer Downtown Washington D.C.

When we finally pull up to the hotel, Rami eases the limo to a smooth stop right at the front. The red carpet is laid out as if it already knew I was coming. He steps out first, then walks around to open my door. He offers his hand, and I take it, stepping out carefully, making sure my dress behaves because tonight is not the night for wardrobe malfunctions. The second my heels hit the carpet, everything feels almost cinematic. Cameras flash, and I feel like a celebrity. I guess my Beyoncé theory isn't too far off.

Before I can take it all in, Ben walks up to greet me. He loops his arm through mine, and escorts me toward the photo area.

"Amina, you look stunning," he says warmly. "I hope you enjoyed the limo ride."

"Thank you!" I exclaimed. "Yes, the ride was amazing. I really appreciate it."

We take pictures, and Ben points me toward another room where OHE & Associates staff are gathering. I thank him and head that way. When I step inside, conversations pause, and heads turn in my direction. You would have thought everyone in the room saw a ghost. *Well, this ghost sure does look good*. After the shock dissipates, the room fills back up with conversations and smiles.

I greet the people closest to me first, some familiar faces, some not so familiar.

"Amina, it looks like you put together an amazing SPARK," someone says, nodding with genuine approval.

"Ms. Ali, you look great tonight," another adds.

I smile and thank them. Tonight, I'm allowing myself to receive. Then I see Lucas. He approaches without delay, hands firmly in his pockets.

"Hey, Amina," he says. "Everything looks great, and so do you."

"Thank you, Lucas," I reply, as I survey his face. I'm surely surprised to hear this from him.

After the greetings die down, I take a seat and wait for Ben to come in and brief everyone. I glance around the room again, casually at first, then more deliberately. There's still no Donovan.

For reasons I don't fully understand, butterflies appear in my stomach. I'm both excited and nervous to see him tonight. I shift in my seat, take a breath, and remind myself to keep my composure.

Finally, Ben comes in and gives us a quick briefing. He walks us through the flow of the night one last time, but more than anything, he takes a moment to tell us how proud he is. Not in a corporate checkbox kind of way, but sincerely. He knows all the hard work it took to get us here.

Then we head into the adjacent room where the happy hour is already in motion. The space is alive with conversation and soft laughter, drinks pouring, and glasses clinking. I float through the room, making small talk, and exchanging pleasantries. I'm present, engaged, and doing exactly what I'm supposed to do. Then, I see him...

Donovan stands across the room, looking just right for the occasion. Ben said dress appropriately, and he sure did exceed those expectations. Every line, every angle, every inch of him was carved with intention. He's dressed in a way that is effortlessly grown and sexy. Fitted brown corduroy slacks cling to his thighs just enough to make it impossible not to notice his quadricep muscles. He has on an elegant blue blazer that sits perfectly on his shoulders. His haircut is crispy, a clean low, drop fade that sharpens his already dangerously handsome face.

He flashes his eyes at me for a few seconds. He lifts his glance slightly, a quiet acknowledgment meant only for me, then smiles and gives a small wave from across the room. I feel my mouth curve into a slow, intimate smile before I turn back to the conversation in front of me.

After happy hour winds down, we transition into the main ballroom as planned, for dinner and the presentation. I watch people laugh over plates and enjoy their food. Chef Dion really did his thing. Seeing everyone enjoy their food makes me happy. It's one more piece of evidence that the night is falling into place exactly how I envisioned it. I eat, but barely, more aware of the moment than the meal. My nervousness begins to increase as the evening inches closer to the part that belongs entirely to me. The part where I have to get on stage and speak in front of hundreds of people.

Once I've had enough food, I excuse myself from the table and slip out of the ballroom. I just need some air before Ben takes the stage and says my name into a microphone. The hallways outside are calmer, the noise muffled, and the lights softer. I inhale deeply and let my shoulders drop. Still, my heart beats a little faster than usual with the weight of the eyes and expectations pressing in on me. I'm walking further away from the ballroom.

I don't get far before I feel Donovan's presence. He stops me and reaches for my hand, lacing his fingers through mine, and for a moment, he doesn't say anything. He just looks at me, his gaze going up and down. From my face to my dress, to the way I'm standing there trying to hold it all together. Then he just smiles.

"What," I ask, suddenly self-conscious, my voice coming off more aggressive than I mean to be.

"Amina... woman," he says quietly, shaking his head like he's in disbelief. "You look stunning."

"Thank you," I reply, nicer than before, my eyes dropping for a half second before I look back up at him.

He studies me a little closer now, almost as if he can see past the dress and the makeup. His expression changes from amazement to concern.

"Hey," he says gently. "You look concerned, Amina, what's wrong?"

I exhale. "I'm just... a little nervous about my speech."

He nods, understanding immediately. "Okay, that makes sense." Then he leans in slightly, lowering his voice. "How about this... I'll stand off to the side of the stage, so it'll be like I'm right there with you."

I look up at him.

"If you get nervous," he continues, "just look at me. We'll do this together."

Before I can respond, he lifts his hand and gently tilts my chin up, forcing me to meet his eyes. His gaze is reassuring me that he's there for me.

"Amina," he says, "everything you're about to hear tonight, every bit of praise, you earned it. You did your damn thing."

I feel a knot in my throat. I neither trust myself to speak nor do I know the right words to say in this moment, so I step forward and wrap my arms around him instead. He holds me, solid and grounding, and for the first time all night, I feel like I can breathe again.

But then he steps back. Just enough to create space. Just enough to make me feel some type of way. I look at him, confused, my body still leaning toward where he was a second ago. He reaches for both of my hands this time. His tone shifts to something more serious.

"Amina," he says quietly, holding my gaze. "I know we've been spending a lot of time together. I know we've been... enjoying each other," he says. A small smile comes across his mouth, but it doesn't last long. "All of that has been great, more than great, but I want more."

I just stare at him, not really understanding where he's going with this.

"I want you," he continues. "Not just in moments, not just behind closed doors, I want you officially." He squeezes my hands. "I want you to be my girlfriend."

The world feels like it tilts. I stare at him, my heart screaming yes, but my mouth doesn't move. The words pile on the tip of my tongue, but none of them make it out. Suddenly, my lips part.

"I... I—"

But, before I can finish, Ben's voice echoes through the ballroom. I can hear him calling me onto the stage.

"And now, presenting to you the mastermind behind this year's SPARK, Ms. Amina Ali."

I look up at Donovan, not knowing the right words to say. "I... I have to go on stage," I say, already stepping back, my hands slipping from his.

He acknowledges, eyes still locked on mine. I turn and walk briskly toward the ballroom. My heels carry me forward, but my heart stays behind with him, his question still hanging in the air, unanswered.

I step onto the stage, and the room opens up in front of me. There are hundreds of faces staring back at me. The lights are warm but unforgiving, and for a split second, I feel the weight of every night, every doubt, and every sacrifice standing on stage with me.

I begin my speech and just let words come out. My tone is calm and confident at first, but after about two minutes of trying to keep my composure, my tone changes. The words start moving faster than my brain can keep up. My hands tighten around the microphone. Clearly, I'm extremely nervous.

I glance to the side of the stage, and Donovan is there, just like he promised. He's standing tall, and his eyes are locked on me, like I'm the only person in the room. In this moment, it finally all makes sense. People are meant to choose things that see them, value them, and appreciate them. So why is it so hard for me to choose Donovan, if he's already chosen me?

I stop mid-sentence, and the room goes quiet. I step away from the podium and walk toward Donovan, heels echoing softly against the floor. I reach for his hand and look him in his eyes.

"Yes," I say gently. Not in the microphone, though, just to him.

His smile comes quickly, but I can tell he's trying not to do too much. Before anyone in the audience can process what is happening between us, I pull him forward with me and lead him onto the stage.

I turn to the audience, my voice stronger and fuller, "And I couldn't have made this happen without this man right here," I say, squeezing his hand. "Mr. Donovan Davis."

The room is still dangerously quiet.

"He's been in my corner as my colleague, my supporter, my advocate, my friend, and..." I pause, smiling up at him, "my man."

The room erupts in applause, and for a nanosecond, I feel like I just won *Showtime at the Apollo* and survived the criticism from the audience.

I watch the audience as everyone claps and jumps to their feet, like they just watched somebody win something big. It sounds like affirmation, like relief, like recognition. Donovan smiles beside me, still holding my hand like he's not letting go for anything.

I catch Anna's eye in the crowd, and she's smiling like she just solved a mystery before the detective showed up. I smile back because she definitely had her suspicions, and now she can confirm them. I know we're going to get a kick out of this back at work on Monday.

Then I see my queen.

Grandma Jamila is standing near the back, chin lifted, pride written all over her face like a testimony. The woman who prayed over me and my dreams when I didn't have the language to conceptualize any of that. The woman who made something out of nothing and dared me to believe I could do the same. She's here, and she gets to see this moment with her own eyes.

I squeeze Donovan's hand and take another breath. Standing here, on this stage, in this room built on polish, power, and proximity to whiteness, something else hits me.

I am a Black woman from Amberline Heights. From a place people love to label before they ever bother to understand. From a neighborhood often labeled as *too much*, too loud, too bold, too complicated, and *too Black*. They thought that it meant I couldn't be excellent. They thought my culture was a liability instead of my sharpest tool. They whispered that I was an exception, a quota, and a diversity hire that didn't earn every inch of this moment with my own mind, my own grind, and my own resilience.

But here I stand.

Not because I assimilated. Not because I shrank. Not because I gave up. Definitely not because I softened myself to make *them* more comfortable.

I stand here because I refused to disappear.

I stand here because I turned sacrifice into strategy, doubt into discipline, and pressure into purpose. I carried my people and my upbringing with me and still delivered excellence in a way they can't deny.

Hand in hand with a man who sees me fully, surrounded by applause that speaks for itself, and watched over by the woman who raised me to believe that I could surpass any ceiling they tried to place above my head. I couldn't be more grateful. This isn't just a win, this is proof.

Maybe I am a DEI hire.

I got my job.

I got my apartment.

I got my recognition.

I got my man.

I am Amina Ali.

I Definitely Earned It.

www.ingramcontent.com/pod-product-compliance
Lightning Source LLC
LaVergne TN
LVHW090511110826
845146LV00003B/819

9798995462002